"The historical element . . . is merely the background of a poetic and profound study of the young Indian, Quick Eagle, and his abiding love and respect for his father, the chieftain. Told with a cadence that recalls the simplicity and poetry of traditional Indian legends."—Chicago *Sun-Times*

"It's an excellent portrayal of human relations, and one which will suit the idealism of teenagers."—(Starred Review) *Kirkus Reviews*

". . . a compelling story for teenagers."—Detroit *Free-Press*

". . . the symbolic and meaningful rituals and beliefs of the Indian are simply and movingly put forth through the thoughts of a chief's son, Quick Eagle. Sympathetically and beautifully written . . . should enthrall both boys and girls."—Jackson *Sun*

"This exceptionally fine Indian story will hold the reader, boy or girl, spell-bound. A powerful story."—*North Country Libraries*

"Mr. Doughty knows history. His plot situation is good, his detail authentic and colorful."—*The New York Times*

". . . this author's . . . novel is full of power and depth; and is written in a style which will transfix the reader."—(Starred Review) *Library Journal*

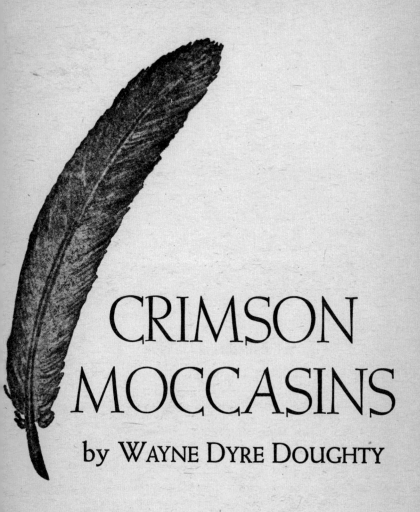

CRIMSON MOCCASINS

by WAYNE DYRE DOUGHTY

A HARPER TROPHY BOOK

Harper & Row, Publishers
New York, Evanston, San Francisco, London

CRIMSON MOCCASINS

Copyright © 1966 by Wayne Dyre Doughty

First published in 1966. 2nd printing, 1966.

First Harper Trophy Book printing, 1972.

Standard Book Number: 06–440015–8

FOR BETTY—

The killer of a lot of little deaths
and the perpetrator of many plagues

Contents

Part One

RED HAWTHORN BERRIES

1777

One

Day of the Warrior

At dawn a gray Miami canoe dog slipped from behind the council lodge. Pausing at the edge of the dance ground, it lifted its head and sniffed. Then, claws clicking on the hard-packed earth, it moved toward a meat rack.

Abruptly the dog gave a bound. Jaws snapped shut just below the lowest hanging strip of drying venison. Up again—*click*—down. Up, down.

Whimpering, the old gray dog put its tail between its legs and trotted forlornly off, its hunger still unsatisfied.

A jay in an elm tree scolded the dog without mercy. A red squirrel hurried down the limb of an oak, changed its mind and ran back. Two owls came gliding in, their big, round, night-hunter eyes a little bleary. One owl winked at the other in a dignified manner and walked stiff-legged down an oak branch to its hole.

In the east a pale pink light began to tint the bottoms of low scudding clouds. The stars in the west gradually faded away. The clear, clean river sang over rocks at the river bend. A mild southwest wind rustled the drying leaves of poplar, oak, maple, and sugar birch. Soon the white wool would shower out of the north, the eye of winter would look upon the Indian earth, the geese would be gone from the sky, and the red berries would leave the hawthorn.

But for now it was Indian summer.

And it was the day that Quick Eagle would become a warrior in the nation.

In the largest bark lodge, beside the meat rack, just as the dog's jaws snapped shut a man opened his eyes. He looked straight up, then all around, and when the boy lying near him stirred a little, the man closed his eyes and resumed a steady, even breathing.

"Aii," the boy said to himself. "It is that old gray dog that wakes us each morning. One day we will put him in the cook pot for his bad manners and I shall sleep until the sun is warm."

Quick Eagle then sat bolt upright in his sleeping robes. He had remembered at last what day it was. He was seventeen, the age of manhood. It was the Moon of Red Hawthorn Berries, the day he would become a Miami warrior. His boyhood was behind him and after eight more days, the period of his Manhood Testing, he could truly say that he was a man. In time he would be confirmed as hereditary chieftain and would become a wise and compassionate leader of his people. As it was with his father, Blue Heron, so would it be with him.

Quick Eagle got up, putting on a breechclout of blue wool that was made in an encircling, skirtlike arrangement. The clout came well above the knees and was fringed on the bottom with a band of fresh-water pearls. He slid his feet into moccasins, which were stiff with crimson beadwork. His mother used exactly the same beadwork design on his moccasins as she did on Blue Heron's. Some mornings Quick Eagle would be halfway out the door before he realized the moccasins he had on were a little large and not his own. His father had a bigger foot. Otherwise the moccasins were the same.

Quick Eagle glanced at his father, then went to an earthen bowl for a drink. There was an insect floating on the surface and he plucked it up and put it to one side. The water had a sharp mineral bite that Quick Eagle loved. His mother used the same spring Feather Wind did. If he married Feather Wind, the water would be the same in the new lodge as it was now in this one. Also there was a good chance that the women would use the same meat rack and throw sticks at the same dog.

Quick Eagle glanced quickly over his shoulder, intending to take his father by surprise. Was the chieftain really asleep? Could it be possible? Would the man who led all of the Miami nation and could influence half of the Shawnee be asleep on the very day his own son was ready to become a warrior?

Quick Eagle groaned. He clashed his teeth together,

several times, imitating the old gray dog. Then he stood still, his young face calm. He had full lips which were tremulous at their corners, brows that were straight and black above hazel-brown eyes, and his lashes were sooty black, as elegantly curled as wild turnip shoots.

"Father?" Quick Eagle said softly.

No answer.

"Father, the morning quickens."

Blue Heron's breathing was regular.

"Father, the old gray dog has come around."

Silence.

"Let us go together, my father. It is time to go. They will be looking for us at the river."

Blue Heron slept on.

Quick Eagle groaned. He thought he might suddenly shout, "Wake up! It is your son's great day!" But he changed his mind. Blue Heron had been known to jump up with a knife in his hand and a Miami war whoop on his lips. He had done it once when Quick Eagle was about seven and took the notion to pull Blue Heron's nose in play. The boy had landed on his back with a sharp point against his chest. Blue Heron cut him a little too, just to teach him manners.

When Quick Eagle was smaller he did many foolish things and his father did not always punish him. Sometimes Quick Eagle had a certain nightmare in which he tried to scream out in terror but could not, no matter how he strained. In the nightmare there was always a pressure over his mouth, and often in the dream it seemed that the pressure was caused by a dry, cold palm.

When this bad dream came to Quick Eagle, he would always crawl on his hands and knees in the dark looking for his father. And, always, Blue Heron gathered him under the robe and held him in strong warm arms until the dream faded. Sometimes Blue Heron would keep him until the stars were above the smokehole of the lodge. Then his father's fingers, as they pointed toward the sky, seemed to go up and move around among the stars, and, together in the night, they would choose the star where they would pitch their lodge when they had died.

His father spoke of heaven as a place where the arrows were sunbeams and where the deer killed with these arrows did not really die.

Watching his father now, Quick Eagle smiled. Then he sobered; smiled again. "It is easy to see a certain son in this camp is unloved," he said. "The father does not care to get up and go with his son."

No answer.

The boy's shoulders rose; he filled his lungs, then let out his breath gradually, making a low, mournful sigh. He looked at his mother. He could make out the veins in her eyelids, as delicate a design as the tracery of a spider's web. Her skin was the color of mellow brown doeskin, and the lightness of it told of her grandfather's French

7

blood. Quick Eagle's skin was as light, but with more of an olive tinge.

Seeing his mother was asleep, Quick Eagle sighed again and turned away. Then, throwing a fourth best robe over his shoulder in a casual manner, he stooped out through the low door and quietly made his way along the path to the river.

Nobody else in the camp was up. In the still gray gloom of dawn the lodges looked like round bark turtles in slumber. He looked for streamers of smoke above the lodge of Feather Wind and her father Hard Knot. He wondered if his best friend, One Fire, would meet him on the sandy beach.

He passed the hut where the white captives were being held prisoner. The man was a Mitchi Malsa, a Big Knife Kentuckian. To the Scalp Buyer at Detroit the hair of the whiteskin was worth five blankets or a musket. The little girl with blond hair and eyes the color of robins' eggs would be adopted by the war chief Many Thunders. The wife of Many Thunders had been sad since her own child died of a strange sickness and she had begged her husband to find a substitute. Many Thunders talked this over with Blue Heron one evening, and the next day took a small raiding party south, to Kentucky.

Quick Eagle frowned when he saw Red Panther's lodge. Red Panther was his rival, and he had been on the raid with Many Thunders. Red Panther had killed a whiteskin man, one who had been helping the two captives in the prisoner hut look for a strayed cow. In the kill-talks around camp it was said that Red Panther had struck from behind.

Red Panther had sewn the blond scalp to his legging seams and paraded where Feather Wind would be sure to notice him. He could take the scalp to the British at Detroit and be paid in trade goods for killing a Mitchi Malsa, but Red Panther preferred to keep the scalp and impress Feather Wind. Also Red Panther kept bringing her father Hard Knot the choicest game and in all other ways made up to him. Hard Knot was old and he was poor and it was well known that he was seeking a son-in-law to be a good provider for his old age.

Yet Quick Eagle would not be eligible for legal marriage for an entire year. He hoped to prove, in his Manhood Testing, that he could be as good a provider at seventeen as Red Panther was at nineteen. If he returned from his eight-day ordeal of the testing with a horse for Hard Knot to ride, it would show Red Panther up. Horses were hard to come by, harder than scalps sometimes, and a horse was something Hard Knot had never owned. Bringing a horse to Hard Knot might be enough to set Red Panther back the full year Quick Eagle needed. Otherwise there was little hope.

Quick Eagle pushed through a screen of willows and came out on a sand beach. He spread his robe and stepped out of his moccasins. Then, stripping off his breechclout, he waded cautiously into the shallows and lowered himself into the water.

"Hii!" he cried. "It is cold! *Cold!*"

He smiled, waiting. Often One Fire would hide and not show himself until Quick Eagle had tested the water. But there was no sign of his friend and no sign of the other youths, and, worse, no indication of his father being aware of what day this was.

Quick Eagle sat gloomily in the shallows, slowly scrubbing himself with sand. He almost pulled his hair into two strands for braiding, but remembering what day it was, changed his mind. His hair was so black it had bluish highlights. It floated behind him like a curtain on the water. The cold, flowing water washed along his ribs. He splashed a little in his face, then, braver, ducked his head under and washed his hair.

"Cold," he said. "It is cold."

He watched the rim of the sun rise above the poplars in the east. The gray shadows in the forest became purple, then blue, then brown. Warm yellow shafts of sunlight patched on fallen brown leaves. A cedar waxwing came to sit on a branch and sing to him: *See me? See me?* Now the leaves on the trees turned silver, and as the wind touched them they rustled, and then he saw their true autumn colors of scarlet and gold. A rich smell of earth rose. He sensed the hint of winter in the smoothly spreading warmth of the day. He arose, dripping, from the water and went for his moccasins and robe.

Then, just as though he shared a secret with the Master of Life, Quick Eagle winked at the morning splendor of the fully risen sun.

He stood silent, wrapped in his robe. By lifting his head a little he could see the bend of the Wabash above the mouth of the Tippecanoe. It was a two-day paddle to the British post at Vincennes, downriver. A good distance upstream was the portage between the Wabash and Maumee rivers, a carrying place the Miami nation controlled, which had sometimes been disputed and fought over by the Iroquois from the East in the days long past.

The first cousins of the Miami people, the Shawnee, lived further south, along the Mad River and the Great and Little Miami rivers that flowed into the Ohio. The principal chief of the Shawnee was Cornstalk, but Blue Heron's best friend among them was Black Fish, who had adopted many sons. One son was a whiteskin—Daniel Boone; another, a taciturn little orphan boy called I Cross Somebody's Path—Tecumseh. Quick Eagle wondered how Tecumseh felt, having a whiteskin for a foster brother.

It was the upstream route and a swing through the Wyandot country that Quick Eagle planned to take on his Manhood Testing. But, for now, he moodily made his way back to the lodge, encountering no one.

Stooping in through the low door, he said, "I am here." His eyes glittered in anticipation of the greeting he would get.

But neither his father nor his mother was even up! They had forgotten all about its being the day he was to become a man and warrior!

Quick Eagle moaned. Water from his damp hair ran down and dripped off his brows, striking his cheeks like tears. His heart was broken. His father had not noticed that the moon had turned last night into the Moon of Red Hawthorn Berries. His father slept on, not knowing this was his son's great day.

Quick Eagle sighed and went to his bed, rolled it up, and sat on it brooding. He got up and walked around with his hands caught behind his back. He glanced at the jar of family water, saw that the insect he had put aside was alive and stirring. It was a bumblebee. Quick Eagle put in on his palm, cupped his hand gently, then stood by the lodge entrance blowing his warm breath on the bee to help dry its wings. And, blowing, he also whistled in an undertone, just like a cedar waxwing, hoping that somebody who cared would hear: *See me? See me?*

Then, suddenly, the toes of Blue Heron's moccasins appeared on the floor beside his own. The chieftain stuck his head out of the door, looked up at the sky. He looked east, around the village, then studied the hills to the west for a moment. He saw the sky, the hills, the camp—he saw everything except that it was the Moon of Red Hawthorn Berries.

"The morning looks good, my son."

"It is a morning," Quick Eagle said gruffly. He opened his palm and released the dried-out bee. It bumbled over his fingers, then buzzed and lifted, and *zip!* it was gone. "Like any other morning, my father," Quick Eagle added. "Father, it is here. That is something good we can say for today."

Quick Eagle sighed. He saw the old gray dog slip from behind the council lodge and pad away into the brown, gloom-gold autumn forest. He felt like that: gray, a dog, trotting forlornly off after missing what he hungered for.

Two

The Chieftain

The lodge fire was like the red eye of a slumbering gray dog. Quick Eagle's mother knelt and put dry grass against the single coal, blew gently, and a yellow-red flame jumped up and the grass caught. Adding twigs, then two hefty sticks, she soon had her kettle boiling. Quick Eagle and Blue Heron stood patiently by the lodge entrance, one to either side, as she went back and forth between them for meat and firewood.

At last she signaled to them that it was time to eat. Blue Heron sank smoothly to the floor to sit cross-legged. Quick Eagle imitated the graceful motion. He sat with his own legs crossed, facing his father. The knees of the two men almost touched.

The woman placed the pot between them. Then she looked Quick Eagle over. "Did you bathe, son?"

"The water was very cold, Mother. My skin was like the flesh on a goose."

"Hmm," she said. She inspected behind his ears and in them. Quick Eagle put down a wail of despair and showed his hands, palm and knuckles. He showed his elbows, then threw his father an anguished look. He was still being treated like a child.

Blue Heron looked gravely on.

Quick Eagle's mother ran a calloused finger over the line of Quick Eagle's jaw. "I feel one," she said when she came to his chin. She got her clamshell tweezers. Quick Eagle held his face up to her. Lately she had been doing this, pulling out tiny stiff hairs.

He winced when his mother yanked. "It was a big one this time, Mother. I think it was attached to a tooth."

"They are very ugly, my son."

"Pull them out, Mother. I am very brave."

"Perhaps your face will grow full of them, my son."

Quick Eagle stared at her. And stared. Then he laughed. "What a brave man I will become then!" he cried.

He turned to his father. "Ho, my father. Listen to her. She would have me hairy-faced like the whiteskins." He chuckled. "Perhaps they will be red hairs like those on the face of our captive."

Blue Heron lifted dark, somber eyes to Quick Eagle. "Perhaps, my son, the white man believes that the face hair makes him handsome."

"Ae, my father." Quick Eagle laughed. "He looks like he might be trying to swallow a porcupine."

Blue Heron said nothing.

Quick Eagle looked at his father a little shyly. "Did

your mother pull yours, my father? As my mother does mine? It is like torture."

Blue Heron lowered his eyes. "For you, my son, a little torture is nothing."

Quick Eagle leaned forward from the waist, white teeth gleaming in his grin. He put his hand on his father's knee. "I believe my mother likes to torture me," he said in a mock whisper. "Father, she has a heart for such a thing. If the council votes to torment our white prisoner, Father, I think my mother's heart would let her light the fire."

Blue Heron smiled a little. "All hearts are made in a room the Great One has. Perhaps he distributes them without much discretion. Perhaps this is the greatest thing of all. We are only children of the Master of Life and must use the hearts he gives us."

Quick Eagle blinked. "Father, I do not understand what this has to do with torturing a white prisoner."

"Eat, my son. You are thin."

Quick Eagle bent to sniff the contents of the pot. Blue Heron exchanged a glance with his wife over the top of the boy's head. The woman clacked her clamshell tweezers at her husband, then sadly shook her head. Blue Heron closed his eyes and nodded slightly. He opened his eyes then, and his eyes said to her, "Someday. Not now." The woman frowned at him. She stood behind Quick Eagle and pointed to his unbound black hair. She indicated Quick Eagle's broad back. She held her hand nearly six feet off the floor to demonstrate his size. Blue Heron only nodded, then looked down to where Quick Eagle's fingers still rested on his knee.

Quick Eagle dug into the pot and came up with a chunk of deer meat on his knife blade. He ate without dribbling gravy or making mouth noises. He imitated his father's way of eating. "Father, there are red plums in with the meat."

Quick Eagle smiled at his mother. She would wait to one side until the men had finished. It was the same with all mothers in the nation. "The meat is good, Mother. It is very good."

"A certain son shot the deer. Perhaps it is the flight of the arrow he tastes."

"No, Mother. It is the meat itself. It is in the cooking. It is very good. We will save some of the plums for you, Mother." Quick Eagle lifted his eyes to his father. "This tastes especially good in the Moon of Red Hawthorn Berries. The deer meat is sweeter at this time. And the plums."

Blue Heron pursed his lips, appeared to consider it unlikely the moon affected the taste of the meat.

Quick Eagle sighed. It simply had not occurred to his father that he was seventeen this moon. Perhaps it would occur to him tomorrow. He resigned himself to defeat. He sat, eating slowly, mentally casting himself into the mold of his father, mentally laying plans to be just like him.

Blue Heron was one of those who did not take to adornment, being partial neither to feathers nor bright blankets nor elaborate quillwork on his leggings and buckskin shirts. He was dressed this morning in a Miami clout of red wool and in the red-beaded moccasins like Quick Eagle's own. His hair was long, black, unbraided; it hung to the small of his back. A copper wrist guard glimmered on his bow arm. There was a blue, snakelike tattoo on his bronze chest.

Blue Heron held himself with an exquisite, leisurely dignity at all times. He had marvelous dark eyes in concave shallows under the brows: eyes that saw buffalo where there were none, eyes that visited in glades where one spoke to the Master of Life and received answers, eyes that seemed to be using the answers endlessly.

With all of this, Quick Eagle was surprised his father had not seen the turn of the moon. Everyone else had seen the nibbled moon come to full circle last night. But Blue Heron only sat, eyes downcast, a slight frown on his face.

The men having finished, Quick Eagle's mother came to take the pot away. Blue Heron looked up at her and cleared his throat.

"Wife," he almost barked in command. "Fill thy water jar, then eat with some friend. The men of this place wish to smoke."

Quick Eagle slowly lifted his head. Had he heard wrong?

Blue Heron said, "Fetch a pipe, my son."

"I—" Quick Eagle coughed and drew himself up erect. "You wish me to smoke a pipe with you, my father?"

"Those who nibble the moon have consumed the old one. A new moon has been put out for all to see."

Quick Eagle's eyes began to glow. He touched his father's knee lightly with his fingertips. "Ae, my father. I thought you had forgotten me."

Blue Heron leaned from the waist. He placed his hands on Quick Eagle's upper arms, and then he stroked downward, from the shoulders to the elbows, four times, in love and respect and kinship.

"It is hard giving over a son to the world. It is hard seeing the children become men. It is hard seeing you leave us. We do not want you to go."

"But, my father, I am not going away. I will be here."

"It will not be the same, my son. In a time to come you will feel your independence. You will not ask our advice. In a time to come you will marry. You will complain when we wish to visit you."

"Aiee, my father! It could not be true!"

Blue Heron smiled, just a little. "Fetch the pipe, my son."

Quick Eagle rose. He saw his mother quietly leaving the lodge. "Eat well, Mother," he called after her.

He found the pipes and selected the best one. It had a white stone bowl with a long stem painted red and black. Two eagle feathers hung from the bowl, which was carved in the shape of the open jaws of a snake, whose intricate, scaled body encircled the stem. It was the most precious article in the lodge and had hung, unused, for many years.

On second thought, Quick Eagle put that pipe back and took up a simple redstone pipe instead. He handed it to Blue Heron and prepared to sit down, as before, knee to knee.

"I do not accept this pipe. It has a fault."

Quick Eagle started. "Father, it is a fine pipe."

"I do not accept it."

Quick Eagle took the pipe back, hesitated, brought a second pipe of perfectly carved gray stone.

"I do not like this pipe," Blue Heron told him. "It also has a fault."

Quick Eagle considered. Then, moving slowly, he fetched the snake-carved pipe.

"This is the pipe I would smoke with you," Blue Heron said. "Do not bring to me a second best thing where you are concerned, my son."

Quick Eagle lowered his eyes and fell silent. The fire burned on his right. He lifted his eyes to Blue Heron and lowered them again. Coals in the fire fell together with a low hissing sound.

Blue Heron filled the pipe slowly. "Have you considered the day, my son?"

"I have considered it, my father."

"You are sure of this?"

"Yes, my father."

"Think very carefully."

"Father, I have held myself against this time."

"I believe you, my son." Blue Heron handed him the pipe, having lit it and taken the first puffs.

Quick Eagle took the pipe just on the tips of his fingers. His long black lashes held still. His full-lipped mouth was sober. He offered the stem end of the pipe up, down, for Earth and Sky, and to the Four Quarters of the World. He held it to the East Quarter last and longest, for the East was the source of morning and the morning was the dawn of life. He remembered his quiet moment by the river. He remembered winking at the sun. He moved so that his knees touched Blue Heron's knees. He smiled.

"I await you, my father."

"Smoke, my son."

Quick Eagle put the stem in his mouth and gently smoked. He withdrew his lips from the stem momentarily. "I remember, my father. Once you told me I did not have to eat the smoke."

"Good, my son."

"It is very good, my father."

"Smoke, my son."

Quick Eagle smoked. He looked deep into his father's eyes. His still-damp hair curled against his back. A shaft of sunlight coming from the door fell across the wall beyond his father's shoulders. Quick Eagle took the stem end of the pipe from his lips. "It is very good, my father. Father, there is no way that it could be better."

Blue Heron stroked his son's arms from the shoulders to the elbows.

Quick Eagle gently smoked. Then he held out the pipe to Blue Heron. "Yes, my father. It is all very good. Will my father join with me?"

Blue Heron took the pipe from him and smoked it. As he smoked, words came from his lips as softly as the white curling vapors. The words seemed to ride on the smoke and drift in tranquillity with it. With the smoke the words eddied among the furs of the floor, the bark of the walls, the war gear and the hunting equipment, the sleeping robes and the flames of the hearth fire. It was as if the lodge were speaking and the forests beyond the lodge and the creatures of the forest and the music of the river were with them.

"First, my son, there are the eight days of the Ordeal. Have you prepared yourself in mind and body as I have told you to do?"

"Yes, my father. I have prepared."

"Think very carefully, my son."

"Father, I am prepared."

"I believe you, my son. After the testing you must win your way in life as a man and warrior by what character you may have learned from your mother and myself and by your own will. Do you understand this?"

"I will do a great thing on my Manhood Testing."

"My son, a little thing is sometimes enough."

"I wish to do a great thing, my father."

Blue Heron made no reply as he put the pipe aside and stood up with a simple flexing of his legs. Quick Eagle duplicated the easy motion.

"My son, turn your back to me." Blue Heron took his son's hair into his fingers. He slowly fashioned it into a single fat braid which would lie between the shoulders. The braid could not in honor be loosened until Quick Eagle returned from the testing. When Blue Heron had made the braid, he gave it a sudden sharp yank which started involuntary tears in Quick Eagle's eyes.

"This is the last pain I shall cause you as a father. From this time forward you are a man and warrior. I can cause you suffering and pain only as a chieftain. Suffer, my son. I wish it. Only by suffering are strong men built. Weak men are destroyed by the same thing. By suffering a man learns to endure. Be built, my son, and live inward in your heart and soul. Be strong in a thing of joy that will grow inside of you."

Quick Eagle turned to face his father. "And if I am to suffer and be strong, my father?"

"Then you may lend your strength to your people. You can prosper and enrich them."

"As you have done, O my chieftain?"

Blue Heron's lips twitched in a brief smile. "If I am built, O my warrior, then you have put the final vein in

23

my heart. Someday you will find out that I am never so strong as you believe. There are many kinds of strength. Mine is not the most important."

"You lead the host, my father. Other tribes would follow you. It is known that when you were with the Ottawa, Pontiac, that men followed you in battle. That is great strength."

Blue Heron studied the wrinkles over his knuckles. "That was thirteen summers ago. I was very young, very foolish. We lost that war." He flexed his fingers, making fists.

"Someday we will win, my father. We will drive the whiteskins back."

Blue Heron smiled at him. "It is for each man to win his personal battle. I see us, you and me, occupying a time. Let us fill this time with ourselves. Permit your sons to fill their time, and their sons to fill another."

"Council me, my father. I would be as you, completely as you, in my time."

Blue Heron stroked his son's arms. "Be yourself, my fine son. You will stand much taller, much prouder than I. Look inward . . . seek truth."

Blue Heron stepped to the back of the lodge and returned carrying a buckskin pouch. He knelt by the fire, and Quick Eagle knelt facing him. Blue Heron opened clamshell containers that held pigments of vermilion, crimson, ocher, black, and yellow.

Blue Heron painted four bars of vermilion under each of Quick Eagle's eyes with his fingertips. "War, my son. May you be brave. Do not die in a low place, but die on top of a high hill so that you will be seen fighting. When you kill men, kill swiftly. Sometimes the pain of life is enough for a man to bear. I do not believe in torment, my son, for it is no test of manhood to make a helpless man scream. So say I, your chieftain."

"I hear and will obey."

Blue Heron painted a wide yellow line on Quick Eagle's forehead. "Peace, my son. Use it like a weapon and none will die. Keep keen its golden edge. Consider the majesty of the sleeping fawn and the bear cub at play. So say I, your chieftain."

"Ae. I hear and will remember."

Blue Heron painted an elk in black on his son's chest, surrounding it with a crimson circle. "You are an Elk clansman. Remember our brothers and sisters. Share your plenty. Ease the days of the old ones. Suffer it that no child goes hungry because of another's lack. Bury your kinsmen on a scaffold so that the Master of Life need not stoop to harvest their souls. If you are murdered, the scarlet ring of your kinsmen and justice will put to bay the wolf and slay the panther that strikes from behind. Take wounds upon your chest, none upon your back in battle. Do not marry within your clan lest conceit finally rule the clan to the pain of its disappearance.

Bring new blood to the clan, and remember that among women the most beautiful are also often unwise. So say I, your chieftain."

Quick Eagle nodded. Feather Wind was a member of the Turtle clan, he remembered. She looked beautiful to him. But also she was wise. And it did not seem right that she should go to the Hawks, Red Panther's clan. Those Hawks had most of the best of things already.

Blue Heron put aside the paint. He sat back on his heels with his palms resting on his knees. "My son," he said, "mine is the honor to lead much of the nation. I hold in trust the red and blue belt of our fathers who came out of the eye of winter and conquered these lands for us. I speak to you as your chieftain. And yet you are my son. My son, become a warrior of this, your nation, and take a place with the men."

"I hear you, my father."

"And when your father is old, show pity. Feed him tenderly of the strength of your arm at hunt. See his helplessness. Lift his feeble head and give him to drink. Honor his bones, for he grasps you by the ankle and holds you fast. You stand before him and beside him and with him in all things. You will be with him even to that place where the arrows are sunbeams and the deer do not really die."

Quick Eagle fell silent.

26

A long tremor of love went through him for his father's last words. He felt a sudden sorrow for himself. He did not feel ready or qualified to become a warrior. He did not like thinking of Blue Heron only as a chieftain, as he should after the testing. His father's strong, warm arms had always comforted him. His father's understanding and patience and wisdom had always guided him. He did not want it different in his home than it had been. He felt, already, a little lonely.

His eyes filled with involuntary tears. A single tear welled out onto his cheek. Blue Heron, seeing it, reached to take the tear on the tip of one finger. It glimmered there for a moment, a single transparent drop.

"For me, my son? Because I will grow old?"

"Ae, my wonderful father. And for me, perhaps."

Tenderly, carefully, Blue Heron carried the tear upward and touched it to his tongue. "It is very good, my son. It is filling. When you fill me, I am complete."

Quick Eagle reached out. He put his hands on his father's upper arms and stroked them downward, from the shoulders to the elbows, many times, in love and respect and kinship.

"Come, my son. I will walk with you to the end of the village. The sun shines. It is your day. Come."

Quick Eagle continued to stroke his father's arms.

"Come, my son. It is time to go."

Quick Eagle's fingers moved down his father's arms. Down, then up, down again. He had strength in his hands and was able to keep Blue Heron from rising.

"Come, my son. It is time."

"In a moment, my father. In a moment. Father, do not always be in such a hurry. Let me be with you here for a little while."

Three

The Three-Day Run

The day had begun for the Miami people when Quick
Eagle stepped from the lodge with his father. Women
were fleshing hides, scrubbing their cookpots after the
morning meal, harvesting plums and buffalo berries, cur-
rants and nuts and papaws, or inspecting behind the ears
of small children when they came up from the sand beach
of the bathing place.

The men fletched arrows, formed hunting parties,
sorted and bundled furs for trade, mended traps, talked
of war. The young unmarried men were at bow practice,
swimming in the cold river, or wrestling. Quick Eagle
could hear boys shouting as they played football in a
meadow to the north. One player could not kick the grass-
filled deerskin ball through the upright goal posts, so he
tried to pick it up and run it over the goal line for a score.
The other boys pelted him with their fists for breaking the
rules. Only girls could pick up a football and run with it
for a score.

The old men sat and smoked by their lodges in the
warm morning sunshine. Quick Eagle was aware of their

29

smiles, and he tried to match his father's stride and way of holding himself, and the old men smiled wider still. Quick Eagle had a smile himself for certain of the old ones, and especially for Hard Knot. He hoped Hard Knot could see the son of Blue Heron, painted, lectured, and now setting out.

Hard Knot sat by himself, his old gray braids lying forward on his sunken chest. He was weak, and Quick Eagle saw him as one of those whose days he was expected to ease, as his father explained, although Hard Knot was not an Elk but a Turtle. Hard Knot was poor and he mixed his tobacco with sumac leaves so it would last longer. Hard Knot lifted his left hand and moved his fingers in a wave at Quick Eagle. So unexpected was the friendly gesture that Quick Eagle stopped and blinked.

Blue Heron stopped beside him. "Are you thinking of Feather Wind, my son?"

"Yes, my father."

"As a wife?"

Quick Eagle stroked his nose with the tip of his forefinger and looked sideways at his father. "I think of her as a song being sung to me. A song such as our women sing when the hunters come home with many kills. A glad song, my father, and it is very sweet."

"Hmm," said Blue Heron. "Moccasins must be made from the hide of those kills. Songs are a poor thread.

30

Singing is a poor garment. It is hard to cook a melody."

Quick Eagle thought for a moment. "My wants are simple, my father."

"Very simple, my son." Blue Heron's eyes glowed. He glanced at Hard Knot. And although Quick Eagle did not see, Blue Heron moved his own fingers in a brief wave. "I think, my son, that when the time comes your feet will wear the finest moccasins of all. When there is a song a man, even if he is barefooted, feels well shod. Do you wish me to speak to Hard Knot? I am chieftain and if I speak for you it will carry much weight."

"I will speak for myself, my father."

"It is good, my son. If you have trouble finding words, ask me about the ones I used to win your mother. Her father did not like me much, but I overcame him with my words."

Quick Eagle smiled to himself. He walked with a light and happy tread toward the end of the village. He was thinking of the men who had been bundling furs, taking them to trade. To him it seemed that the ability to barter and get a good price for the labor of his trapline would help him win a happy life. The Miami were a nation of traders. They also became fierce warriors in order to protect their trade and they were second in battle skills to no tribe. In the ancient trade wars before the white men came, even the Iroquois were made to appear as little children when they met in battle the terrible Miami, the only tribe the Iroquois failed to conquer or even once defeat. Or so the old men said.

Quick Eagle was lost in thought and failed to see the crowd that began to follow behind him until his friend One Fire stepped to his side. One Fire had eyes that bulged, and his eyelids rounded over them so that, from a side view, he appeared to have hickory nuts thrust behind them.

One Fire was supposed to be ugly. The blackish-brown bumps on his face and shoulders were like the warts on a toad's back. But with his eyes One Fire could make people laugh. He was able to roll and rock his eyes until the beholder was left astonished and dizzy from watching. One Fire claimed he had borrowed the left eye from a wolverine and the right one from a panther; they were not really his, he said, but were extra eyes he could discard and replace whenever he wished.

"Ah," said One Fire in a low, rough voice. "It is Quick Eagle after all. The paint had me fooled." Facing Quick Eagle, who had stopped walking, One Fire did something with his mobile eyes. He rolled one eye far to the left, and the other far to the right.

Blue Heron and Quick Eagle both gasped at the same time.

"That is a marvel!" Blue Heron cried.

One Fire grinned. "I was saving it for something special, my chieftain." He looked at Quick Eagle. "Do not ask me to do it again," he said softly. "It can be done only once in a lifetime, and for a friend."

"It is like magic!" Quick Eagle yelped.

One Fire smiled. "A little magic between friends is a good thing. Especially on such a day as this."

Blue Heron reached out and put a hand on One Fire's shoulder. "I am glad," he said, "that my son has you for a friend."

One Fire's ugly bumps seemed to take on a sheen when he grinned. "We are glad your son is a man today, my chieftain, and we have come to see him off."

Quick Eagle saw many of his friends standing behind One Fire and grinning. He frowned a little. "Ha-hi! Well, last night you gave me no sign that you knew about the turning of the moon. You hid in your lodges this morning and made me feel I was forgotten. Thank you. Thank you. I will remember it. I see none of you as being subchief, second in command to me. Not one of you is worthy, for you still play the tricks of little boys."

"Ho!" one of the boys shouted. "A little joke between friends is a good thing!"

Then, from behind a lodge, came Red Panther and a troop of young braves from his warrior society, the Lances. Red Panther was dressed in his best white deer-skin clothes, and the blond Mitchi Malsa scalp stood out plainly in the fringes of his leggings. Red Panther was an extremely handsome youth and his father had been the former chieftain. But Roan Bear was killed in war and Red Panther was living with an uncle.

Red Panther had come in his courting clothes, to make a joke. He had his courting flute in his fingers, and walking along, he blew a few notes on it to test the tone. All of Red Panther's young friends chuckled. One of them, in mock sincerity, asked how it was possible for an Elk to pick up a Turtle, a thing easy for a Hawk to do. Even Quick Eagle's friends laughed about that play of the words on the clan names. A group of girls and women who stood nearby also giggled. Quick Eagle disliked giggling intensely, and he became furious.

He took a step toward Red Panther, the four bars of red paint under his eyes gleaming. "I shall show you!" he cried. "I will come back from my testing with a horse—not like a certain one who came back after a bear had mauled him!"

It was known that this had happened to Red Panther on his Manhood Testing, and on his chest, when it was bare, were the scars of proof. While trying to escape the rain, Red Panther had accidentally crawled into a cave already occupied by a bear.

Blue Heron stepped to Quick Eagle's side. "What is this about a horse?"

Quick Eagle seethed with fury. He glared at Red Panther. It was in his mind to take that flute away and break it. He took a step toward his rival, but One Fire, grunting like a bear, danced between them. "Ha! Well!" One Fire said. "Red Panther is a warrior who could not smell a bear. I think the bear, smelling Red Panther, mistook him for a brother and embraced him in the cave. Why not?"

Quick Eagle laughed with the others. Of all the youths, Red Panther came least often to the bathing place.

"Oh, oh, oh!" One Fire cried, dancing around. "My friend Quick Eagle is indeed a man! He goes to creep among the enemy all naked and weaponless to steal a horse! Oh, oh, oh! What a brave one he will become!"

Blue Heron took Quick Eagle by the shoulders. "My son, what of this horse?"

Quick Eagle saw that Red Panther was going to blow on the flute again. "I will do a great thing! I must!" he cried.

"A little thing is sometimes enough, my son." Blue Heron's fingers pressed deeply into Quick Eagle's shoulders. But Quick Eagle at that moment glimpsed the little white girl out the corner of his eye.

They were near the prisoner hut, and the wife of Many Thunders, the war chief, had been leading the little girl by the hand. But the girl broke away from her and ran straight for Quick Eagle, hauled back her foot, and kicked him squarely in the shins. Quick Eagle yelped, then picked her up and pretended he was going to bite off her nose. Squealing, the girl cried out, "Painted Injun! Red rip!"

Quick Eagle had learned a few words of English from the traders, and also some politics. "Rebel," he told her. "White Mitchi Malsa rebel!" he said, clacking his teeth in her face.

The girl made a small fist and hit him below the eye. "Red rip!" she screamed. Then, seeing some of the paint on Quick Eagle's cheek had come off on her hand, the little girl thrust out her tongue to taste the red stuff.

Everyone laughed.

Quick Eagle held her in his arms tenderly, as he would a sister. He thought her golden hair as beautiful as the river he had seen that morning. For a moment he stroked the silky fine hair and admired the unusual blue eyes, the color of robins' eggs. The whiteskin girl had a dusting of freckles across her nose and Quick Eagle had never seen anything like them. He touched her skin, trying to feel the freckles with his fingertips. And the girl let him touch her, looking up at his darkly handsome, intense young face with unfrightened eyes.

Blue Heron watched Quick Eagle with alarming intentness. When Quick Eagle looked up at his father, he saw Blue Heron twitch as though stung. The rest of the people around them were hooting over the kick Quick Eagle had taken, and the place was very noisy. But between Quick Eagle and Blue Heron there was a strange silence.

"Father," Quick Eagle said. "Father, I have the strange feeling all this has happened before. It is noisy, yet it is still. Father, it is very odd, this feeling. It is like a dream."

Blue Heron said, "Come, my son. The morning quickens. It is time to go."

Quick Eagle nodded and handed the girl to the wife of Many Thunders. "She is very beautiful, my father."

"Yes, my son. Her new parents will love her as their own. She will have a good home. She is Miami now."

"It is good, my father. It is very good. I am ready now, my father."

Blue Heron went a little way into the forest. Quick Eagle's friends followed, and three of the warrior-society chiefs went along. Quick Eagle would be selected by one of the societies after he had done a brave deed such as taking an enemy scalp. A scalp was proof of an enemy conquered. Any man could boast of his bravery, but a warrior society looked for proofs of valor, and a scalp was like a medal a man had won.

Quick Eagle favored his father's society, the Snakes. A man had to do a very great thing to become a Snake. He had to demonstrate leadership and show that others had confidence in him. The Snake selection was not necessarily made because of battle prowess. Less than thirty men in the entire nation were Snakes. Black Fish of the Shawnee was an honorary Snake, as was Pontiac at one time. Black Fish and Pontiac were the only two men outside the Miami nation to be so honored. But Quick Eagle had no hope of becoming a Snake immediately after the testing and would probably be years in achieving it. He would join Many Thunders' society of the Lances. It meant he would be with Red Panther and his friends, but Many Thunders was like an uncle to him and had asked him if he might not like to join.

When Blue Heron came to a certain spot under a huge black walnut tree, he paused and turned to the group of young men and boys following Quick Eagle. Some of the fathers had carried baby boys out to watch the procession, and Quick Eagle was smilingly aware of the bright, button eyes fixed with fascination on him.

The sun was still low enough to cast long shadows, but soon it would walk higher, and shafts of gold light would strike through the reds and browns of the Indian summer foliage.

Blue Heron lifted his arm, the copper bracelet brilliant on his wrist. "Now a Miami youth goes alone to face his Ordeal. Let us hope his success wins him a place among the men. He goes to Indian Earth with no fire, no weapons, no clothing, no support save the skill of his mind and the strength of his body. A boy goes, a man returns. He has spoken of a horse. If he is caught by the enemy, he will be tortured to death; thus will our enemies have revenge against me and the Miami nation for his thievery. I know my son, if he is caught, will perish. But if he is to die, as willed by the Master of Life, then I know he will die well and beautifully, and that he will be singing a Miami war song when the flames and the pain take him."

To his son Blue Heron said, in a low voice, "Have you thought about this time?"

"Father, I have held myself in readiness."

"Think very carefully."

"Father, I am prepared."

Blue Heron sighed. "I believe you, my son. Go now, but do not profane the days. Do in honor, and in honor you will become my warrior."

Quick Eagle stepped out of the crimson-beaded moccasins. "Keep these, my father, until I come for them." He stripped off his breechclout. He handed it to his father. Red and yellow and black paint gleamed on his slim body. His chest rose and fell with quickening emotion. He touched his father's hand lightly, then turned and moved off, slowly. He walked proudly erect, feeling out the ground a little with his toes before he let his heels drop.

In a moment he was gone.

Blue Heron stood a long time looking after him. His dark eyes were lowered. When he lifted them again, Many Thunders came to his side.

The test of manhood in the Miami nation proved many things. But foremost was the ability to be at once crafty and able. To Quick Eagle's way of thinking, craftiness began well in advance of the fact. He wished to be crafty enough to come home with a horse.

Usually when the youths returned from their testing they sang songs about conquering some animal with a club or rock, or snares made of braided willow or dead-fall traps. No doubt they elaborated much on the simple fact that they had lived off the berries, nuts, and roots that were always available in the forests. Quick Eagle could not see that it was much of a test of manhood to do what any ten-year-old could do at any time. It proved nothing about being able to take care of himself throughout life and also take care of others, such as Feather Wind and her father Hard Knot.

Quick Eagle had diligently worked and carefully collected a bundle of select furs: silver fox, martin, two albino mink, eight excellent beaver, twelve sable from trade with the Chippewa, and a white *wakan,* or sacred buffalo robe, from trade with a Sioux at the fair.

This, all of it, was surely the price of a horse if a Mitchi Malsa scalp was the price of five blankets or a musket.

He headed for Detroit, knowing it would take him three days to reach it. A three-day run, overland from the Wabash, was a good test of manhood. No other man would make such a run in that time except in case of war. Also a shrewd trade would show that he was both wise and crafty.

When he had spoken to the British traders at Detroit

40

early in the summer about trading for a horse, they were eager for him to come. They said Governor Hamilton, the Scalp Buyer, would welcome him. These British traders called Quick Eagle "the Portuguese" sometimes, or "the Cajun" because of his olive skin and long, elegant, sooty-black lashes, which Indians did not usually have.

Quick Eagle did not know what the words "Portuguese" and "Cajun" meant, but he suspected the British said them as a compliment because he was the son of the chieftain. They always smiled when they used these words, and he knew the British were eager to be friends with Blue Heron. The British wanted the Miami to go to war against the Mitchi Malsa Kentuckians in the south. So the British, eager to please him, might trade for more than a horse. He would like also to have two mirrors—one for his mother and one for Feather Wind. And if he got a third, he could see better to get those tiny stiff hairs out of his own chin. His mother was cruel with those clamshell tweezers, and, besides, Quick Eagle did not like the way she was always clacking them behind his back at Blue Heron.

Quick Eagle found his cache of furs undisturbed. He caught the weight of the pack over his shoulder. As he ran he shifted the bundle every so often, from left shoulder to right shoulder and back again. He was sorry One Fire had blurted out that he intended to creep among the enemies for the horse. He himself had said no such thing—only that he intended to return with a horse. One Fire often said things on impulse to amuse others and did not give much thought for the truth of matters.

Quick Eagle went as swiftly as he could that day. He splashed through rivulets and streams, ran through forests so dense the sunlight seemed never to touch the ground save when fall and winter came and the trees were bare. The leaves fell around him, and the colors he saw were astonishingly beautiful. He saw the deep maroon of dogwood, the golden maple leaf, the shimmery copper of oak and the crimson of sumac. A few evergreens gave vibrant depth to the splendor of the golds and reds, the yellows and the plum maroons.

He smiled as he thought of the plums in the bottom of his mother's cookpot. He thought of how his mother sat to one side while he and his father ate, knee to knee. He knew that he and his father would each eat a better breakfast if she ate with them; for both he and his father left the choicest morsels in the cookpot for her. When he sat down in the morning with his own son someday, he would leave the best of the meal to Feather Wind, his wife. And his son would do the same.

Quick Eagle wept a little at that thought. He wondered if, one day, his own son would stroke his arms downward from the shoulders in love? He could see his little son sitting there, wanting to be a man. He would be gentle with his son, as Blue Heron was always gentle with him, and he would live in a happy lodge all his life.

He wished for this happiness with Feather Wind; it was his dream. And when he dreamed, he did not have the nightmare. Sometimes when he was fully awake the nightmare would come. He did not understand what it meant, except that there was violent death. Sometimes he saw children being killed, and to escape the vision he would run or swim until he was exhausted; and what he did not want to remember was put aside. But eventually the nightmare would come again. He was very small in the nightmare, and he was held tight, and there was the dry, cold palm over his mouth. . . .

Birds lifted into flight ahead of him. Once he saw a deer with dripping muzzle at the edge of a stream. Twice he saw grouse. A marsh hawk skimmed along above the treetops off to his left. On the right a whirlwind of quail burst from cover and threshed the air with a brown-white *whirrr* of wings.

He came to a stream and did not see a way to cross. Then, running along the edge of the steep banks, he made out a fallen log that bridged the stream just ahead. He stopped long enough to shift his pack to the other shoulder.

He paused for a moment on the log and looked back. He could no longer see the smudge of smoke above the trees that indicated the location of the Miami village. Still on the log, brown naked, he felt the sun striking across his cheeks. His paint glistened. His slender body glowed. His eyes softened and he breathed deeply. He felt like a man. He rejoiced in the strength of his body. His long limbs, light brown and slim and supple, glistened with his sweat. He felt he would make a good warrior. He was a boy before, but now he was crossing this log into the silent beauty of the autumn forest to manhood and warrior things. He smiled, throwing back his head. The soft weight of the single fat braid lay between his shoulders. He remembered how his father yanked his hair. He remembered his own wink at the Master of Life by the river earlier in the day.

"Ae and ae," he said. "It is truly my day. The sun gives me power and lights my path."

He left the log and began to run again. He ran, smiling, forgetting time and distance, forgetting everything except the full, fierce joy of running.

And at dusk he selected a briar thicket and crawled in on his belly, dragging his pack of furs with him. He found a place of dry grass under the thorns and lay on his back. No animal would venture into the briars to disturb him. No enemy would think to look here. He did not smell a bear.

He waited for night.

And, waiting, he thought about the little white girl with the sunshine hair. How beautiful she was. And how strange. First she kicked him and called him a name, then, when he held her, she remained quietly in his arms. In that moment he felt such a great affection for her, an affection he had felt only for his father and his mother and for Feather Wind before. How odd that was. And how oddly Blue Heron had looked at him. It was the only time in his life that Quick Eagle was shocked by something in his father's eyes.

Something lurked in Blue Heron's eyes, a thing he had not seen before. It was uncertainty. It was a flame of doubt. It made Blue Heron seem weak. Quick Eagle had never thought of his father as being weak, except in that one brief moment. Even now he wasn't sure he saw in Blue Heron's eyes what he thought was uncertainty, doubt and weakness. It was odd. Very odd. And oddest of all was the sudden knowledge that there were things, perhaps many things, that he did not know about his own father.

Quick Eagle settled in the grass and tried to sleep. He pillowed his head on the furs. He watched the stars appear. The stars became warm points of light, so bright, so low, Quick Eagle thought he might be able to touch them. It was very warm, and the night was extraordinarily clear.

"Ae and ae," he said. "I must sleep. I must get a better start in the morning than I did today. Also I must remember that the old gray dog will not be coming around to wake me up when he jumps for our meat."

He crouched on his toes, doubling his knees against his chest. He put his chin on his knees and grasped his ankles with his hands. He tipped back, then forward, back again; toes to heels to toes. Slowly he rocked. And, rocking, he sang.

> The wind blows over me.
> I feel I am swinging,
> On a tree bough
> In my cradle board.
> My mother will catch me
> If I fall . . .
> O wind, blow over me once more . . .

Singing, rocking, tilting slowly back and forth, eyes closing, he at last toppled over and was sound asleep.

Four

The Judgment

When he awoke it was daylight. He was in a glade at the edge of a scarlet sumac thicket. There was a stream nearby and a small meadow. He crawled from the briar thicket with his bundle of furs and went to the stream for a drink.

The water was not the mineral water of the spring, but it was good. Good! He saw a small fish scoot from under a gray-green boulder on the stream bottom. Lichens on the rock swayed when he reached downward, trying to catch the fish with his fingers. He buried his face in the water and rubbed his nose on the slick green lichens of the rock.

Lifting his head, he scrubbed his face with his hands, worked his fingers into his ears to clean them, and rubbed his face to dry it. He discovered one of the short stiff hairs his mother tried to pull out from time to time. He worked at it, but he couldn't get a good grip on it to make it come out, so he let it alone.

He looked down at his reflection in the water. He lay very still. He saw the fish come back to its place under the rock. He smiled, then had another drink. He held water in his mouth, then tipped back his head and swallowed it down.

Suddenly he sensed that all was not well. His heart was gripped with fear. He felt the presence of people in the clearing with him. Yet he went on drinking, in full view of the hidden, watchful eyes. These were enemies. They would torture him to death as his father warned. He must have been careless. But he would not die here, between hills. Lifting his eyes, he looked for a big rock or broad tree to protect his back. He fumbled for the lichen-covered stone on the stream bottom, the only weapon he would have. The fish scraped over his arm, getting away.

Then hands gripped him by the legs and shoulders and he was jerked roughly to his feet. He looked into the hot, angry eyes of a thoroughgoing man of war.

"Many Thunders!" Quick Eagle cried in relief.

The war chief of the Miami inclined his head. He had a grim jaw, eyes set wide apart above a crooked nose. His lips were drawn in a thin, white line. Behind Many Thunders other warriors of Quick Eagle's tribe stepped into view.

"We have slaughtered a deer, Quick Eagle," Many Thunders said. "Perhaps you would like to eat with us?" Many Thunders jerked his head toward two men, who brought forward a deer haunch.

"Yellow Wolf," Quick Eagle cried. "Two Strikes. Buffalo Horn . . ." He stared at them wonderingly.

"Eat," they told him. "You must be hungry."

"But I cannot eat!" Quick Eagle shouted. "You know I must find my own food lest I dishonor the testing."

"Oh, yes," Many Thunders said. He motioned with his hand. Four men came forward and grabbed Quick Eagle. Others ripped open the bundle of furs and scattered the pelts as if they were looking for something. Quick Eagle was dragged to a tree and lashed securely.

He was so surprised he could only gape at them. The warriors did not seem to want to see him but kept their eyes averted. Their faces were solemn, even sad. They flung the furs in the pack every which way.

Many Thunders barked an order and the warriors began to gather dried leaves and twigs. One knelt to strike flint and steel, beginning a fire. Quick Eagle looked at the fire. He looked at Many Thunders and back at the fire again. He strained against his bonds, but was unable to move anything but his head.

"My father will kill you for this!" he cried.

Many Thunders gave him the merest of glances. Then he kicked at one of Quick Eagle's furs near his foot. He picked up a silver fox pelt and dropped it into the fire, watching it burn. It sent up an odor of scorched hair, then a rancid, oily smoke. One after another, Many Thunders added furs to the fire until they were destroyed.

"Feed the boy," Many Thunders directed.

Before Quick Eagle could make an angry retort, two men stepped up to him. One clutched him by the jaws while the other put a sliver of venison in his mouth. The

49

first man made him swallow by punching him in the stomach.

Quick Eagle was numb with bewilderment. They continued to stuff him with food, and as he sagged against the rawhide lashings it came to him they were officially breaking his testing by making him eat food he did not get for himself.

Then Many Thunders stepped up to him. "Where were you going with the furs?"

"They are not stolen. They are mine!"

"Where do you go? Why?"

Quick Eagle stared at him. "Why do this? You are like an uncle to me."

Many Thunders barked at him: *"Where? Why?"*

"To—to Detroit to trade for a horse. But—but you have burned them!"

Many Thunders groaned. "So it is true. You were not going to steal a horse from the enemy?"

"No. I—"

"Untie him," Many Thunders said. "Wash him off in the stream. Give him something to wear."

When Quick Eagle was clothed, they trussed him up like a captive, tying his hands behind his back, putting a thong around his neck to lead him by. They led him off into the autumn forest, toward the village of Blue Heron.

It was night when they came to the village. No fires were burning in the camp, but through the doorways he saw the lodge fires which glowed like burning, reproachful eyes. He was jerked along, in disgrace, toward the council lodge. Inside, he could sense that the place was filled with people; he could hear them breathing. But it was dark, very dark. He stumbled over outstretched legs as did the two warriors guiding him along.

They reached the end of the long house, where the darkness was thickest. Someone behind him began to undo the single fat braid Blue Heron had made. His hair fell free, and he was pushed to the floor. He felt his clothing being jerked off. They covered him with an old buffalo robe.

The silence lasted a long time. It was a thick, breathing silence that grew in intensity. Quick Eagle heard a slight shuffling of feet, a few muffled coughs. Black despair filled him. He lay quivering.

What had he done?

And why had they undone his braid?

He dared not move from where they put him. He dared not ask the questions burning his lips. What had he done? Under the robe, in the darkness, his eyes shot from side to side like those of an entrapped wolf.

Then he heard a mumble of voices from the direction of the door. He sensed that somebody had entered and was walking toward him. He heard people shifting positions, making room for another to sit down. These sounds were just in front of him. He looked, unseeing, in that direction.

Blue Heron spoke. His voice was heavy, slow. He seemed to be speaking from a long distance away, and there was a quality of defeat in his voice.

"I am glad you have made it dark in the place of judgment. I cannot see your faces. You cannot see mine. There is much justice when the accused and the judge do not have to see the faces of others that are concerned. I thank you for this, my kinsmen."

"Oh, my father," Quick Eagle moaned. "What have I done?"

"It comes to us now and then," Blue Heron said, "that one of our young men cheats on the day of his Manhood Testing. Such has happened here again, this day, with another."

"Father!" Quick Eagle cried. "I did not cheat! I—"

"The testing of manhood," Blue Heron said in a low voice, "is to show that we are men of nature and live at the discretion of the Master of Life. We send our young men naked into the forests because we believe it is a new beginning for the man and that he should come into this second beginning as he came into the first: at the discretion of the Master of Life. It is a simple way. We can only believe that violaters of this simple way have chosen to show that they do not have to depend on the bounty of the Master of Life but can survive by themselves.

"At times," Blue Heron went on, "the Master of Life does not return to us the young man sent before him.

52

Perhaps he has found a lack in the young man and puts something in the forest that will destroy him. This is the will of the Master of Life. Perhaps the Master of Life has great love for the young man before him and takes him to the place where the arrows are sunbeams. We cannot know why some men do not survive the Manhood Testing. We are men, with little wisdom beyond the simple ways our fathers taught us. The one here before us we must judge as men. We cannot judge as gods."

Quick Eagle began to weep under the robe.

"This youth, long ago, was seen to be hiding goods. Yet we are a people who live without locks and bars on our doors. The one who saw these goods being hidden gave the information to the council, and the informer also suggested a reason for the hiding of the goods. Whatever the motive of the informer, it is done. We gave the one before us a full day to get rid of his furs. He did not do this, and it betrayed our confidence in him. It would be the same if he had buried some weapon to make his testing easier. He sought to buy his way before the Master of Life, not earn his way. He sought to purchase a place in nature, not accept it. We cannot tolerate this act and keep faith with our fathers, who showed us our way at the time of our beginning manhood. For eight short days we wish our young men to remember Mother Earth and to go out to her, naked like a child, and come back to us and our society, a man. All our young men must be shown examples of wrong thinking when it occurs. So say I, as chieftain."

Quick Eagle had not understood that the furs were a compromise with the Master of Life and tradition. Now he felt his guilt fully for the first time. He quivered with shame. The silence in the council lodge was a living thing, a coiling serpent that sapped his strength and destroyed his thinking.

Blue Heron raised his voice. "We will hear from the accused."

"I wish to die!" Quick Eagle wailed. "Oh, kill me for my great failure."

"The punishment is for you to be banished, forever, from this nation. Banishment from our lands and from our tongue and from the lodges of the Miami for all time."

"No! I wish to die! It is my right! Let the young men learn from my disgrace."

"The Council has decreed banishment. And so say I, as chieftain."

"No," Quick Eagle cried, sobbing. "I plead. I beg. Let me wipe my dishonor away. I claim the right of the Circle. Let me do this. I beg—"

"It is his right!" a voice called out. "And it is a brave thing!"

"I claim the right!" Quick Eagle shouted. "I claim it!" He moved his hands in the dark, touching Blue Heron's moccasined foot. Blue Heron withdrew his foot. Quick Eagle caught it again. Then his father's fingers, in the dark, forced his hands away and Blue Heron withdrew the moccasined foot again.

"It is well," the voice of Many Thunders said. "Go before the council lodge and await us. The circle will be made."

Quick Eagle found his way, groping through the dark long house. He felt the hands of his friends come out to touch him as he passed, to show that someone would remember him after he was dead.

Quick Eagle was surprised that so many hands came out to touch him in the dark. And with each touch a name. ". . . Red Dog . . . Horse Standing . . . Black Club . . . Yellow Wolf . . . Straight Tree . . ." on and on and on, one after another.

When Quick Eagle at last reached the door of the long house, somebody embraced him. He felt the rough warts of One Fire's face on his cheek. He clutched One Fire, and with his fingers felt the quivering lids over the big, ugly eyes.

"Ah, my friend," Quick Eagle whispered. "I tried to look two ways with one pair of eyes and could not do it. Good-bye, my friend."

One Fire's voice was choked. "I know who informed the council. I know who saw you bury those furs. It was Red Panther. He has always been jealous of you. If his father had not died, he would be the son of a chieftain. I will kill him for you. Before sunrise he will be dead."

"No, *no!*" Quick Eagle patted One Fire's rough shoulder. "I thank you, but no. No, my friend. The fault was in me, not Red Panther."

"They would not have followed you if you had kept quiet about the horse. If—if I had not shouted out—"

"No, no. It is my fault. It is all with me. Do not blame yourself. My father took a long time yesterday morning to try and make me realize I had certain responsibilities. I would not listen. I tried to look two ways with one pair of eyes. I tried to see Feather Wind and my father at the same time. It would have been the same had I returned with a horse. I wished to buy my way. My father is right. Good-bye, my friend."

One Fire wouldn't let him go. "We . . . did not think the chieftain . . . the council . . . would do this much to you. That banishment . . ."

Quick Eagle shook his head. "Especially to me must my father do it." He patted One Fire's shoulders again. Then, breaking free, he pushed through the door of the council lodge and found a clear space on the dance ground and stood there, waiting.

One by one the men of the village came from the long house. They stepped away into the black shadows of the night. They did not look his way. They went into their lodges and lashed the doorskins tight. Many Thunders was the only one who did not go into a lodge that Quick Eagle could see. Many Thunders stood behind a tree directly opposite Blue Heron's lodge. Yet Quick Eagle was sure that Many Thunders thought he was unseen.

Quick Eagle waited a long time before Blue Heron finally came from the council lodge. He was the last to leave, and he stepped out, carrying the old robe which had concealed Quick Eagle while his father gave him judgment.

The village was silent. A low whispering wind was at the smokeholes in the rounded bark roofs. In the night, somewhere a puppy began to whimper, and the tiny voice of a child scolded it.

Quick Eagle, seeing Blue Heron approach him, stood with his arms at his side and his head bowed. Blue Heron walked to within inches of him and stopped, holding out the robe.

"It will get colder, my son."

"Is it allowed, my father?"

"I say it. It is your—" Blue Heron's voice broke off. Then he said, "It is what we will bury you in."

Quick Eagle took the robe and fastened it around his waist. "I thank you, my father."

"Do you?"

"Yes, my father. Many times yesterday morning you tried to show me that the days of the testing were serious and grave. You asked me many times if I had given it my thoughts. I was too filled with myself to listen. I have shamed you, my father. And I have failed you. But I will not fail you again."

"I do not wish your death, my son. Why did you not take banishment?"

"Father, you are the center of my soul and heart. How can I step away from my soul and heart? I love you dearly, Father. I love you even more than I love my mother."

"My son—" Blue Heron's voice cracked, and Quick Eagle knew he would not care to live long enough to hear it crack that way again.

"Hold me, my father, for a little while. When you hold me, I am not afraid."

Blue Heron gave a little cry and grasped him tightly. "Ah, ah, my fine son. Now I kill you. You are going to die because of my pride."

"No, my father. Because I forgot your pride." Quick Eagle began stroking his father's arms, downward from the shoulders. "You make me more a man because of it than I deserve, my father."

A harsh sob came from Blue Heron. And he broke free of Quick Eagle's arms, turned, and strode off. Quick Eagle saw Many Thunders step from behind the tree and follow Blue Heron into his lodge. After a moment the door flap was jerked shut, and nothing stirred in all the village.

Then Quick Eagle was aware of a movement near the council lodge. "Ae and ae," he said. "It is that old gray dog that wakes us each morning when he jumps for our meat."

Quick Eagle pulled the old robe tighter around him, then settled to the ground.

He waited.

And, waiting, he wept.

ᗩᗩᗩᗩ*Five*

The Circle

The circle was nine feet across, drawn in the center of the dance ground. Quick Eagle could step over it, crawl beyond it, erase it with his foot; it would become as though it never was. But the invisible walls of the circle were as high and as thick as though covered with layers of tough elkhide, and they were held together by the sinews of honor. It was the Manhood Testing intensified. It was the Ordeal severalfold.

It was a fast until death.

The old men sat smoking, warming themselves in the sun, and spoke gravely of other youths at other times and their ordeal in the Circle of Shame. None had lasted so long as to will themselves dead. Driven half mad by the smell of cooking food or the sound of running water, they had always crawled out of the circle and been killed with a blow from a tomahawk.

Quick Eagle had been in his circle for four days now.

The young men came to look down at him with hooded eyes. They watched his skin shrink and shrivel. They watched his chest rise, fall, rise, fall again, and saw his blackened tongue and the white flecks that came to his

60

lips. With his blackened tongue, breathing slowly, unmoving on the dirt, Quick Eagle would pry the white flecks loose and chew and eat them. After the fourth day he rarely moved.

He lay in a knot in the center of the circle. He kept himself covered with the buffalo robe and lay with his cheek on his arm looking toward Blue Heron's lodge. The robe was thin and full of holes, but it was all he had and he clutched it to him. He did not feel cold or hunger so much as gradually fading strength. From hour to hour a little more of himself would be gone. Time melted away his reason, crumbled parts of his memory, destroyed areas of his will. Sometimes he believed he was standing up, running rapidly in one place to keep warm at night; yet he could no longer stand up and he knew it.

Sometimes he would dream. He would arrive in a strange place, quite alone, and find himself strolling through a woods or along a path that went down to a river. Once he found himself able to know why every blue flower was blue, why certain of the birds sang a certain way, what made the grass so green, why the deer had no gall, why the beaver's tail was hard, how high the sky was—he knew more than he would ever be able to share with anyone. He knew the secrets of the Master of Life and was unafraid.

Then he did not know these things anymore and was frightened.

He moaned and rolled over on his back. Daring to open his eyes to the sun, he marveled that it had not changed. It vibrated and pulsed and throbbed with a brilliant white light, just overhead. It was very warm, the sun. He remembered the sun from other times when it was as bright and as warm as this. He heard birds chirp. He saw wedges of wild geese flying across the sky. He could hear the clean, clear river singing over rocks at the bend. He realized his rational thoughts were returning. They came and went, sometimes in bright flashes, sometimes gradually, like weather changing.

He was lucky the warm weather was holding. It looked like rain overhead. That might mean the cold would come soon, that the eye of winter would descend, that the snow would cover him where he lay.

But it was going to rain first and he could drink.

Excitement ran through him at the prospect of water. His black tongue was like a buzzing black rattlesnake in his throat. The snake buzzed, sounding a little like a bumblebee he had held in his palm one morning while waiting to be a man. And, buzzing, the snake spoke.

". . . six days now. No food. No water." The snake sounded like One Fire. Quick Eagle had never known One Fire to lie before. But it was four days, not six.

Secretly Quick Eagle had been digging. He was starving now, but the thought had come to him that he would find some worms in the earth. He dug under the robe with his fingernails. He had to be secretive about it because they might take his food away when he found it. He was too weak to go much farther than a finger's depth in the hard-packed soil, but it did not stop him from trying. Hunger was in him like a rabid animal; then it was in him like a dead and decaying animal. . . .

"Did you hear him speak?" It was One Fire's voice.

"No," Red Panther said. "His lips barely moved. I think he is dead."

One Fire shouted, "You killed him! You put him there! I should kill you for it!"

"Kill me, then," Red Panther said. "He should have taken banishment. Many Thunders says he is not one of the people, truly, and is a white."

"He is Blue Heron's son," One Fire said.

"But a white, Many Thunders says."

"He may have been a white once," One Fire admitted. "But they washed him free of this when he was first brought here. None in the village sees him as other than Quick Eagle, son of Blue Heron, and he is not a white. His blood is red. It is the color of a man and it is all that I see. You are jealous of him because of Feather Wind. You struck him from behind as you struck the whiteskin. When Quick Eagle is dead, you will demand his scalp I think!"

Red Panther's tone was serious. "It is true, I did not like him, but I never thought he would ask for the circle.

Two nights ago I went to Blue Heron. I told him that I had cheated on my own Manhood Testing. I told him that I had a knife hidden, and that is why the bear did not kill me in the cave. I told the chieftain I wished to be punished with Quick Eagle. I said this was so because I hurt him, our chieftain, more than I have hurt Quick Eagle. Blue Heron put his hand on my shoulder and looked into my soul with those eyes of his. And he said to me, 'It is good that my son in his pain can touch another man's heart. Your confession has made a man of you. That is much for my son to do, to help another be a man.' "

Red Panther looked down at Quick Eagle. "I hope he is dead soon. He suffers so. Feather Wind weeps in her lodge. Hard Knot has gone into the forest and we cannot find him. I wish to be one of the singers of Quick Eagle's name. I do not want to see him crawl out of that place and be killed like a dog."

"Then," One Fire said, "I pray with you, brother."

On the seventh day of the fast to death, it rained. Quick Eagle lay with his eyes shut and his mouth open, waiting. But not a drop hit him, although he was convinced the rain fell on the back of his throat. He gagged, as though the sweet flood of water threatened to drown him.

The voices he heard buzzed more like rattlesnakes than bees. His mind was sharper now. A thing was growing in him, tall and fine, deep and wide. It was a well-spring of resistance—very calm, golden. He knew himself better than he ever had before. He knew what he was capable of. He could go on for days if only he could drink some water.

He did not know that warriors stood over him with a taut-sewn buffalo robe, deflecting every drop and giving him no rain.

"He has lost his mind at last," came the voice of Many Thunders. "None could expect it to be otherwise after living in such a place for so long."

Quick Eagle then realized he was getting no water. He turned in despair and put his face against the ground to weep. But no tear could form. Then he felt moisture and pushed his drawn, hollow face along a thin muddy trickle, lapping with his black tongue. He chortled with greed. He ate mud, selfishly. He tried to hide his treasures of food from the selfish eyes around him. He held the robe so they would not see.

A warrior spoke, his face grave as he watched the feeble efforts of the boy. "It comes to me that those born white make the best Indians. They have . . . more . . . in their brains. They are not smarter, not more intelligent; they just have more capacity. They are never quite satisfied. It is in them to excel. They are never lazy. It would be good to have his strong blood in this nation. My brothers, I am sorrowful he is dying."

"Yes," said Many Thunders. "He is like Blue Heron in many ways. I have not thought of him as a white for many years. He does not look white. One is always seeing him as a reflection of his father. He is just Quick Eagle, no other. I will never forget how we found him: clutched tight, for many days perhaps, in the arms of a dead white man. It was after the whiteskin fort, Venango, was destroyed in the Pontiac War. Brothers, the Seneca who destroyed Venango could not call themselves The Men of Men that day. They were like dogs, killing whites with their very teeth. And my friend Blue Heron took this child in his arms and told us he was going home. It was enough, he said, the day at Venango, and he wanted to go home with his son."

"White?" Quick Eagle thought. "Killing whites?"

Quick Eagle groaned. He clutched at white things. He gathered an armful of white cold snow and buried his face in it and ate it. He plucked wild honeysuckle and sipped a single drop of sweet white nectar from each blossom. He ran to a white dandelion to blow the downy wisps onto a white breeze slanting in from white clouds. He found the white stuffing in milkweed pods, and ate the delicious white flesh of catfish.

He raised himself up on his elbows, his face muddy and his hair wild. He laughed like a wolf. He was impaled on the sharp white point of a star. His blood ran out of him, white. White flecks were on his lips. White spots danced in front of his eyes.

He heard people crying. They were screaming then, from inside the walls of a fort. They screamed because they were all fighting and dying, but he was not able to scream with them. He saw himself picked up, and a man jumped over the walls with him. The man ran through the forests. Finally the man fell. He lay there, waiting. The man grew cold. Still he lay, waiting. He was close to a stream and he was thirsty and hungry and was held back by those cold, dry hands.

"Ah, ah, ah," Quick Eagle said. It was the nightmare again. He couldn't stand the nightmare.

He began to crawl. He wanted water from the brook, and the cold hands were not holding him now.

> Oh wind . . . blow over me . . .
> . . . tree bough . . . swaying . . .
> . . . mother . . . catch me . . .
> If I fall . . .
> Oh, wind . . . once . . . more . . .

He thought of the thing they would do to him if he crawled out of the circle. He had asked to die to wipe out the blot on his father's honor. But the tomahawk would be cool and cold for a moment and he did not care.

He crawled out of the circle after eleven days.

Hands grabbed him. He sat bolt upright. Cold pebbles of fear were on his brow. He screamed. "Father! I am dreaming. It is the nightmare again. I am afraid!"

He crawled on his hands and knees, looking for his father. Over and over somebody kept saying, "Must not

67

crawl out of the circle . . . must not . . . must not . . ."

He crawled and found his father.

Blue Heron enclosed him in warm, strong arms.

"Father, all the people are dying. Father, they are swinging the little children by the heels and their heads are being crushed against the log walls. Father, they will take me next. Father, I do not want to die."

"Am I in your nightmare, my son?"

"Oh, no, my father. I do not see you there. Protect me from the others, Father. You are strong, and I am weak. . . ."

"You are my son. Sleep now. I will hold you safe."

"Ae, my father. When you hold me in your arms I am not afraid."

His mind whirled away in a fog. He was crawling, crawling. He was swayed like grasses in a south wind, back and forth, back and forth, crawling. He fell, crawling, into a black pool and was spinning in crimson whorls. His hands dropped to his side. Something cold and wet struck his forehead. He felt the lifeblood running out of him. It was white. White.

"Ae and ae," he said. "That is why I suffer so. It is my great sin. I am white. Oh, I am not the son of my own father."

68

Six

The White

Quick Eagle opened his eyes. He was in his own home with the familiar curved ceiling of bark and the smoke-hole above him. His own fine buffalo robe warmed him; the thin one was gone. And instead of the cold earth, there were soft furs under him. His hunger and his pain were gone. There remained only numb weakness and thirst.

And there was plenty of water. He heard it on the bark roof, dripping down the outside walls, tinkling into pools, running. "Water," he croaked. "Please, please, give me to drink."

Blue Heron, who knelt beside him, lifted his head. An earthen water bowl touched Quick Eagle's lips. He drank greedily. It was the good water from the spring.

Blue Heron lowered his head and stroked Quick Eagle's forehead with a damp cloth. "The fever will soon be gone," he said. "He is sleeping now."

"Give me that cloth," Quick Eagle's mother said sharply. "You are awkward and clumsy with it." Her eyes flashed at Blue Heron.

69

He handed over the cloth, but scowled at his wife. "You say that because of what happened. What would you have me do? Refuse him his right to die? He committed crimes against our traditions!"

"Crimes," she snorted. "He was trying to make you proud of him. He wanted a horse to show you he was able to do something special. He is too gentle to be a killer—like you—and could think of nothing else. He is a boy with a boy's heart. And you let him go into that—that circle."

"He is no boy," Blue Heron told her. "He taught us several things about manhood. He was able to starve himself, nearly to death! He has the quiet courage of the true man."

"Yes," she snapped. "And except for a pack of young boys led by One Fire who appealed to the council, he *would* have died. Yes, and many of the warriors who follow *you* made the same appeal. But *you!* What did *you* do? Sat and moped and cried like a tiny baby while Many Thunders comforted you!"

Blue Heron looked sullen. "My son is able to inspire other men to act in his behalf. He is a leader!"

"Oh," she wailed, throwing up her hands. "Leader! Ha! Well, I noticed Many Thunders spoke in your behalf to the council. You, a leader, would not say a word yourself to save your son. Perhaps the women should get together and make the men elect Many Thunders chieftain! Your heart is like ice!"

70

"Woman!" Blue Heron roared. "Do you doubt my heart for my son? My lot is one of example. I could not go to the council and show favor to my son!"

She snorted. "And you call yourself the chieftain. Ha! You are like a small, fat-cheeked baby. A leader of men. Well, I laugh at it. You would have denounced your council for him and you know it. One more day and you would have picked him up and run into the woods with him and we would never have seen either of you again. Well, why not go anyway? Many Thunders can be chieftain."

Blue Heron jumped to his feet. "Wife!" he yelled. "It is the privilege of men to beat their wives with sticks! While we are speaking of traditions, think about that one for a moment."

She handed him a chunky stick of firewood and gave him a defiant look.

Blue Heron looked at the stick, then dropped it on the floor. Softly he said, "It was not my son who committed the crime. It was a thing of the white man in him. I cannot hold him to blame. The whites think of paddlers, not paddling. They think of eating meat, not hunting for it. They think of fire, not warmth. They wish to purchase ease, not earn it. I have seen it in them often. You see how the British are trying to buy Indians to fight their wars for them? It was this thing, the white in him, that was doing the thinking. My son is blameless. My son emerged from that circle, and now he is a man. He is truly my son now. That is why he did not die in the circle. Not because his friends begged the council. He is a strong, true man, and the nation cannot afford to waste him! Many Thunders spoke for me."

"There is white in me," she said. "And I think sometimes of having my work done for me. Why do you not take a second wife and make my work easier? While we are speaking of traditions, there is one for you to think about. I can sit weeping in the lodge while the second wife does all my work for me. Perhaps Many Thunders knows of somebody who will want to marry you. Shall I send him to ask around?"

Blue Heron's eyes flashed. Then, suddenly, he smiled. "I did not make you my wife because you had some white in you or because you did not. I have found nothing in you that is contemptible to me."

"There!" she cried. "You have just said that because he is a white was no reason for saving him! The council was made to save Blue Heron's son, not somebody blameless because he is a white. Let me sit on that council, and I will show you how to handle people. A woman should be chief!"

Blue Heron roared, "I will never understand you! First you condemn me for punishing him, then you blame me because he was not allowed to die!"

Blue Heron turned and started to stalk away. Then, turning back, he growled at her, "You cannot keep him a boy forever. Someday he will have to be a man. And then he will break your heart!"

"*I! I!*" she cried. "It is not I who coddle him!"

Blue Heron made a gesture of disgust and swept out of the lodge.

"Drown in the rain!" she called after him. "See if I care!"

Quick Eagle's mother applied the damp cloth to his forehead and smoothed back his hair with her hard, calloused hand. She crooned softly to him, an old cradle song about the wind. Quick Eagle, in a half slumber, heard the song far off, as if in a dream. And over the song, drifting in and out, were his father and mother and their angry words.

He opened his eyes. "Mother?"

She closed his eyes with her fingertips. "Sleep, my son. Regain your strength. I will make you fat again, never fear. In the morning you may have wild sweet potatoes basted with raccoon fat. And bear meat. And son—son, I will kill a dog for you. Would you like that?"

He touched her hand. "Mother, I am not a child."

"You are your father's man," she told him. "But you are my child. Sometimes I think that I have two sons, for your father is like a boy once in a while."

Quick Eagle watched her a long time. But she was not really his mother. And Blue Heron was not really his father.

"Mother, why am I here?"

"Because you are loved. When there is love, then you are here. For a long time it was lonely, but then there was love and you came to me."

"Why do you love me? I am not your son."

She drew back. "Please, my son. Please. You are stabbing me. Do you wish to twist the knife in me now?" She covered his eyes with her palm.

"Mother? Mother, do you weep?"

"Yes, my son. You have stabbed me."

Quick Eagle wept. He remembered the little white girl on the day he went to the testing, and how Many Thunders had stolen her to substitute for a lost daughter.

"Aii," he said to himself. "I am a substitute son. I am nothing to myself. It is not me but a lost son that they love. They see this lost son in me. I am a lie to them and to myself."

He thought now about how his parents had deceived him. He was dark, he had dark eyes, his hair was black, and they thought he would never find out he was a white. He did not have the blue eyes of the little white girl to remind them. He did not have her sunshine-yellow hair. The people would always understand that she was a white. They would be kind to her; Many Thunders and his wife would probably love her, but she would always be different and always know it. He had never known he was different until now.

Bitter lines formed in the corners of his mouth. His

74

eyes held a lurking darkness. He felt contempt for his artificial parents—then suddenly contempt for himself. He was something apart from his people but living with them. He was an outsider, a substitute. He had no identity anymore. He was not Blue Heron's son. Blue Heron would not let him die an Indian—had saved him because he was "different," an "exception," a white—A Mitchi Malsa whiteskin!

He remembered the British traders calling him "Portuguese" and "Cajun." Was that his true tribe? What of his clansmen? Was the white girl a clansman? Was the white captive man with the red beard his brother? His uncle? Who had he been among the whiteskins? Was he the son of a chief? Who *were* the Portuguese and the Cajuns? Who was Quick Eagle—really?

He recovered slowly. One by one, and in pairs, the young braves—and some of the old men—came into the lodge to see him. The old men sat and smoked and told him how well he had done to claim the right of the circle, to fast until he was almost dead. They shook their heads, marveling, and smiled upon him.

Quick Eagle suffered them patiently until they went off.

Red Panther came, even before One Fire, and knelt at his side and stayed there silent for a long time. Quick Eagle, propped up, kept his eyes averted from Red Panther. He would not look at him.

Red Panther finally said, "It was I—behind your back."

Quick Eagle said nothing.

"They found Hard Knot," Red Panther said. "He came home."

Quick Eagle said nothing. He was surprised to hear that Hard Knot had been lost.

"Feather Wind does not weep now."

Quick Eagle said nothing.

Red Panther said, "I heard you asking the traders about the price of a horse. I guessed why you were burying the furs. I told the council. I am the cause of your sorrows. I bring you a gift. I wish that we, you and I, can start over in a new way."

Quick Eagle heard these words with suspicion. He turned his head, saw that Red Panther no longer wore the blond Mitchi Malsa scalp on his leggings.

Red Panther unwrapped the deerskin bundle he carried and revealed the finely carved courting flute. "This is all I have to give."

Quick Eagle shut his eyes. "I shall never marry."

"Feather Wind—"

"It was a passing thing. To make you jealous. I shall never marry."

Red Panther's eyes rounded. "But—"

"Please. I wish you to leave me. I do not want to talk about it. Take the flute with you. Be happy. Use it. I give it back to you. I shall never marry."

"But, brother—"

Quick Eagle turned his face away. He blinked back tears, and bit his quivering lips. He would never be able to face Feather Wind again. How could he go to her if he didn't know who he was? He had been robbed of his identity. Would he go to her as the son of Blue Heron, which he was not? As Quick Eagle, the white substitute for the man she might have married? How could he go to Feather Wind and be honest in all things? He could not. He would never marry.

Quick Eagle wept.

One Fire, for the first time, looked ugly to Quick Eagle. One Fire brought some hazelnuts and walnuts and sat cracking them with a war ax, putting them on a little bark dish. He was patiently working out the nut meats, and Quick Eagle knew he was building up to some joke. One Fire was laboring hard to be funny, for he still held himself partly to blame for Quick Eagle's troubles.

When he had finished with the nuts, One Fire put his large rough hands on Quick Eagle's chest. "Let me feel the earthquake of your great heart," he said. "It is like the kernel in a big nut, all red with sweetness. We will eat some of these lesser kernels, and maybe the spirits will grow an oak in us to make us valiant. In me, anyway. I am a coward, after all."

Quick Eagle breathed deeply. "Does the tremor of my earthquake frighten you?"

"Ae and ae. Such a thing would shake the forests if it

were to escape. Oh, my friend, you were so great. Just to lie there on the earth and die. Oh, oh, oh! It was so beautiful. You shrank up like a persimmon. Your eyes looked like those in a long-dead wolf. Your skin turned yellow, then black. Your fingers were like bones. Oh, oh, oh, it was all so wonderful to see. Everybody wept."

"Yes," Quick Eagle said caustically. "I noticed that. They drank water I could have none of. They ate food I could not taste. They laughed and would not share with me—"

"Nobody laughed!" One Fire cried.

"They wanted me to *die!*" Quick Eagle fixed One Fire with a harsh stare. "I heard *you* say you would pray for my death."

One Fire stared at Quick Eagle. "But wasn't it what you were trying to do? That you could fast until you died to wipe away the dishonor to the tradition of the Manhood Testing?"

Quick Eagle smiled grimly. "I did not die. I am alive in the name of nothing."

One Fire shook his head. "I am confused. You *say* nothing."

"I am white!" Quick Eagle cried. "White!"

One Fire blinked. "You are a Miami. You are Quick Eagle, son of Blue Heron, friend of One Fire the coward."

Quick Eagle grew irritated. His eyes narrowed, glittering in slits like a wolverine's. "I wish you to be my blood brother. You can . . . share my great heart. Since you admire it so."

One Fire looked surprised. "Wonderful. I hope for it. We will be brothers—always." He got out his knife and slit his palm, poised the knife over Quick Eagle's palm, slit again. Then they pressed their palms together and called each other brother.

"Wonderful," One Fire said with a grin. "I feel brave already."

Quick Eagle smiled thickly. "Now you are part white."

"Now Blue Heron is my father, a little," One Fire said.

Quick Eagle chewed his lip. Then he said quietly, "Is the white prisoner still here? The man?"

One Fire cocked his head. "White prisoner?"

"He too is a brother to my blood. I wish to speak to my brother. Is he still here?"

Now One Fire frowned. "You tricked me. Why?"

"Has our exchanged blood not made us heart brothers? I wish to speak to the white man. Is he here?"

"But—why?" One Fire cried.

Quick Eagle turned his head away. "I have lived a lie. I am not an Indian. I am not Blue Heron's son. I am a substitute. It is . . . painful—to be a secondary thing."

"You are Blue Heron's son!" One Fire insisted. "A great Indian. Second only to your father! My brother, fifty youths stepped out in your defense. They begged the council to let you out of the circle. They slashed their skins and bled for you. They said they would chant your name each night after all the council lay down to sleep. They would make you a ghost to haunt the nights. They are your friends, your people. And this is your home. You are Blue Heron's son. If ever a man had a home and a people, these are yours."

Quick Eagle turned his head away. "The white man is dead then?"

One Fire sat in silence for a moment, hand over his eyes. "He is a camp slave. He hauls wood and water for the women."

"I wish to speak to him. When I am well again, I wish to see him. You must help me. You are my blood brother, and I do not want anyone else to know when I go to the white man."

One Fire moaned. "You have never been sly before," he said. "You have never been secretive. I am not sure the blood you give me is good blood. But I will do what you say, when you are ready." One Fire stood up. After a moment he left.

Quick Eagle did not know why he wanted to talk to the white captive. He was not sure he would be able to. Lying there for many days, thinking, he could not recall anything of his whiteskin life. He remembered no faces or words, but then he realized that he had always had an easy time learning English words from the British traders. Now he knew why this was so. And he knew now that they had known he was a white. Even the little blond girl, when he held her in his arms on that morning of the Manhood Testing, must have sensed it. You could fool men, and nations, and you could even fool yourself, but you could not fool a child, or not for very long. . . .

And Quick Eagle had always felt *something*. That somehow he was trying to remember something and could not. All his life it had been this way, and when he tried to remember what it was he forgot, he recalled only the nightmare. Shutting out that scene of horror, he shut out everything else. He did not even want to think about it now.

He was angry that Blue Heron had not told him he was a white. He tried to think of the life he would have had knowing he was white and still being Blue Heron's son. He could not imagine it.

His mind whirled in confusion, doubt, anger.

Four mornings later Quick Eagle sank to the floor to sit before Blue Heron for the morning meal. For days he had watched Blue Heron, studying him point for point, looking for some kind of a sign that Blue Heron had changed in his attitudes. He saw no change whatever.

Blue Heron acted as if nothing had happened—as if life could be resumed just as it had been before he left for his Manhood Testing. The man Blue Heron confounded the boy. He was the same now as he had always been, but Quick Eagle found *himself* changed—he had been cruelly hurt and the hurt had changed him.

Quick Eagle could not face Blue Heron's eyes anymore. He pulled back a little, head tipped forward, knees not so close to Blue Heron's. He did not cast himself as Blue Heron's son, into that mold of aloof dignity, and did not meet his mother's eyes.

"Did you bathe, son?"

"Wife!" Blue Heron barked. "Our son is not a child!"

Quick Eagle's mother snorted. She ran her finger over the line of Quick Eagle's jaw. "I feel one," she said.

Quick Eagle almost wept. He caught himself just in time. "I am very brave, Mother. Pull it out." He lifted his eyes to Blue Heron once, and had to bite his lips to keep them from trembling.

He ate glumly, in silence.

"We will share a pipe, you and I," Blue Heron told him. "I have some news to tell. The Snake Society wishes you to become a member."

A Snake? Quick Eagle's blood leaped. A Snake? Their society was the most highly respected, and the most mysterious, in the nation. A man had to do a very great thing to become a Snake. What had he done?

"They have agreed," Blue Heron went on. "You are the only man to survive the circle."

Quick Eagle's heart sank. Coldly he asked, "Did I survive it?"

Blue Heron raised his dark eyes to the boy's face. For a long moment Quick Eagle looked into his father's eyes, seeing only gentle inquiry. He glanced away. Uncontrollably he shivered, as from an icy wind.

"Do you have the nightmares, my son? You are trembling."

Quick Eagle stared coldly at Blue Heron. "They live with me stronger than ever. I feel there is great truth and significance in the nightmares."

"Bad things cause bad dreams, my son. Good things cause good dreams. Your nightmares are very rare now. When you have them, I will comfort you."

Quick Eagle almost leered at his father. "If I am a man, a warrior, and no longer a child, then I do not need comforting."

Blue Heron said gently, "I am a man, and you comfort me. If there are enough good things, then the bad will leave us. Neither you nor I will have nightmares again."

Quick Eagle's lips parted in amazement. "You have nightmares?"

"When you have them, then I have them. When you are wounded, I bleed." Blue Heron reached to stroke his son's arms.

But Quick Eagle jumped to his feet and stalked out of the lodge. He did not want Blue Heron to touch him, ever again.

One Fire volunteered to guard the door of the prisoner's hut one evening and Quick Eagle slipped in. He had not seen much of the white man in the past days. The man, naturally thin, was now almost gaunt because of the scanty meals they gave him to keep him from having the strength to escape. His buckskins were smoke-blackened and torn, and the Indians gave him no footgear. Otherwise he was not treated badly and had become a familiar figure around the camp. The white man seemed content so long as he could keep an eye on the little white girl, and know that she was not harmed. Sensing this, the warriors told him they would kill the child if he tried to escape.

The whiteskin was unbound, asleep under a good fur robe. Quick Eagle hovered over him for a good long while, studying the man's bearded face. The beard was red and matted with twigs and burrs. He rubbed his own jaws, wondering how soon the fullness of the hair would overcome him? He knew his mother had only been pulling out the start of it.

He clapped a hand over the whiteskin's mouth to warn

him not to cry out suddenly. The white man's eyes opened instantly, green as a grass snake. The white man felt the prick of Quick Eagle's knife in his side and lay still.

Quick Eagle leaned close. "No noise," he said. "I take away knife. No make a noise."

The white man nodded. Quick Eagle held up his knife in plain view, then settled back on his heels. He watched the white man for a long time before he spoke again.

Abruptly he said, "I am white."

The green eyes lit up. "Good boy. You want to escape? That it?"

Escape?

Quick Eagle faltered. "I do not know. Maybe." He thought for a moment. "If I go—escape—you take me to white man's place? You tell me about parents?"

The white nodded eagerly. "I'll take you to Jamison Station, in Kentucky. Kentucky—you understand? Near Harrodsburg. Many presents for you. New rifle, cloth, beads—anything you want. Help you find your family, as God's my witness."

Quick Eagle watched him with hooded eyes, squatting on his heels. "Maybe not escape. Maybe we burn you up. You are a slave. Not worth much."

The white man raised his chin. "Do anything you please. I ain't afraid of anything you can do."

Quick Eagle grunted. "Maybe I am not white. Maybe I just come to fool you."

The white man hesitated. "I seen you out there in the dirt. I got close one day and you were moaning in English. You were saying things a little white child would say. You're white. You got an English cast to your features. I think maybe you're part Spanisher or Italian. Them long black lashes just don't grow on Injuns, boy. Spanisher, I'd say. Spanishers are dark, a lot of them."

Quick Eagle did not understand everything the man said. He caught the part about the English cast, though. "I British? British live in Detroit, not Kentucky. British hate Kaintuck. Maybe I go to Detroit."

"No, no, no!" the white man cried. "You're Kaintuck! Don't you remember nothing?"

"You know"—Quick Eagle looked sharply at the white man—"Venango?"

"Venango? Boy, wasn't nobody got out of that alive. Was in sixty-three. This is seventy-seven. That's fourteen years ago. Everybody was killed at Venango, they said. But that for sure makes you an American. That's close to Fort Pitt. Nowhere near Detroit or the British."

"You telling true?"

The white man nodded. "When we going?"

Quick Eagle shrugged. "I not go. It is all a lie I tell you."

He stood up and looked contemptuously down at the white man. Then he turned and swept out into the night.

86

One Fire caught him by the shoulder. "What did you find out?"

"Much," Quick Eagle answered. He was a "Spanisher" from Venango, near Fort Pitt—was an "American" and an "Italian" and a "Kaintuck" with an "English" cast to his features. "I learned much," he repeated. "I am everything, all at once, and no Indian." He twisted away from One Fire and walked off, more confused than ever.

"Red blood," One Fire called after him. "It is the color of a man."

Quick Eagle stalked toward the council lodge. He was being made a Snake this night, and despite everything was excited about it. Because it was an event of importance, he had taken pains to dress well. He wore an eagle feather at the back of his head, sloping downward and canted to the right a bit. His gray leathers, the shirt and leggings, were painted with red stars and blue moons. His clout was red wool. His moccasins were stiff with crimson quillwork. He walked slowly, toes down first and then the heels.

It was while he was passing under the elm tree opposite Blue Heron's lodge that he heard a faint cough. He turned and was startled to see Feather Wind step from the shadows. Drawing himself up tall, he said hoarsely, "It is not seemly for a maiden to walk this way. The maidens wait at home in case suitors call."

Feather Wind came closer to him. "I waited, but you did not come. I wondered about you."

He shrugged, looking away. "It is well known that I am still alive. You must have eyes and ears."

"Yet I did not see you come. And I do not hear you there, whistling like a cedar waxwing, when I go for water to the spring."

"Sometimes I would follow you," he admitted. "But not close."

"You no longer think of me?" she asked.

He turned a little, looking over his shoulder. He could see the lovely line that was the bow of her lips. Sweetgrass scent from her braids wafted to him on the still evening air. "I do not think of you," he said. He tugged at the fringe on his buckskin shirt.

"Do you hear the song of another?" Her voice was like a summer wind among the cornflowers. He saw a faint glimmer on one of her cheeks and a misty light in her eyes. She turned her head quickly away so he would not see the tears. He trembled in love for her; she heard his sigh; he stepped close to her; she leaned against him, and he put an arm around her waist.

"I stand in a dark cave, Feather Wind. I see nothing, it is dark. I hear nothing, it is quiet. I am alone and lost. There is no song in my cave."

"In the old times the ancient ones lived in caves," she said. "If they were together, it was a home to them."

He touched her hair lightly with his lips. He wished to touch the tears upon her cheeks with his lips, but he dared not.

"My cave is damp and gloomy. No fire would warm it. It is not a good place to live."

"I will sing. My song will echo in your cave. Follow my song to the light once more. Outside the cave we can make a home and laugh at what is behind us."

He smiled down at her; she smiled up at him. She came only to his chin. His eyes filled with involuntary tears. He loved the round top of her head so.

"The cave gives no echoes," he said. "I do not hear."

"Let me sing louder," she said shyly. "I am singing now. Do you not hear?"

He stroked her arms, lightly, with his fingertips. "I must not listen."

She tugged, firmly, at the fringe on his shirt. "Open your ears. The song is sweet. I did not make it. It was made within and comes unbidden to my lips. It is my heart singing. It is an old song, but a new song too. Can we not sing it together?"

He held her tenderly. His nose moved in her hair near the center part. He desired to rub her nose with his nose, but he dared not. Her warm breath on his throat made him weak. His love for her made the moment very sweet. He wished to stand with her forever in the warm autumn evening, but he could not.

"It comes to me that I am not worthy of your song," he said. "Why not sing it to another?"

She put an arm around his waist. "It is our song. It is not for others."

"It is not seemly for a maiden to walk this way. The men sometimes are made weak. They cannot help themselves."

"It is the way of a maiden to follow her path. She sometimes cannot help herself. On my path there is only you. I see no other."

"Do you not see Red Panther? He is not so bad."

"He makes music with a flute," she said. "But the song is not so sweet. My heart hears your song."

He whispered, lips near her ear, "It is not seemly for a maiden to walk this way."

She tugged at his sleeve. "My father awaits your coming. He says the courtship would be short, because he almost lost you once. He likes you and says we can be married in two years."

He smiled down at her. "Does he?"

She smiled up at him. "Perhaps, he says, only one year. He likes you very much."

"We will see," he said.

"You will come to him and speak?"

"Soon. Soon," he whispered. "I will come, in my time."

"I will wait."

"And I will come. Soon. Soon."

90

She withdrew her arm from around his waist. "I have not acted properly," she said.

"Nor I." His arms slipped away from her. "But I am not ashamed. I am proud."

She smiled, then moved away, lost among the shadows.

He went, sighing, toward the council lodge.

Seven

The Snake

The long house had a council fire burning, and at the far end sat the Miami sachem, the medicine man, called Rising Owl. He sat quietly, smoking his pipe. To his left was an elderly warrior that Quick Eagle had not seen before, and on Rising Owl's right was another stranger, a younger man than the first. The three men were bare above the waist and their Snake tattoos showed on their chests.

Quick Eagle felt nervous. He looked into the glittering eyes of the men and apologized for being early.

"It is a good quality," Rising Owl told him. "Do not apologize for coming first."

Quick Eagle nodded. "Thank you, wise father."

The man on the left, in a magnificent buffalo robe which was folded over his legs, looked up at Quick Eagle. "It is said that you stayed eleven days in the circle. It is said you had only a spark of life at the end."

Quick Eagle nodded again. "It is so. But the people fanned this spark and I know life."

"A good answer."

The man on the right spoke. He was a man with round

black eyes and a large nose. "We hear that you have the loyalty of many friends."

"I hope the loyalty is not misplaced," Quick Eagle said.

"A good answer."

Rising Owl smiled. "Sit down, my boy."

Quick Eagle sank to the floor, crossing his legs. He knew now that the two strangers were chiefs. Both came from distant Miami villages and were probably of the Wea or Piainkishaw or Eel River divisions of the Miami tribe. They had come because the British were expected to arrive the next day. Tomorrow the Miami would hold a conference to decide whether to join the Shawnee and the Iroquois in a war against the Mitchi Malsa in Kentucky and other white men far to the east beyond the mountains.

Quick Eagle did not know what the council had decided about general war, but he knew that Blue Heron had been with the council discussing it for many days. Quick Eagle knew that if he left with the white man it had better be before the decision for war was reached. The Miami might burn the white captive if the council voted for war. Some warrior, in his wildness, might even try to injure the little white girl. If she was harmed, Quick Eagle made up his mind then and there, he would kill the man who did it.

Many Thunders arrived with five local Snake Society members and took a seat beside Quick Eagle, leaving one man to be custodian of the door. Although Many Thunders was at the head of another society, the Lances, he was a Snake as well. Many Thunders, Quick Eagle noticed, had an odd-looking knife in his belt. The blade was filed to look like a snake fang. No other man there was armed.

Then Blue Heron came in. He wore a snow-white leather shirt and leggings, a crimson clout, and scarlet-beaded moccasins that matched Quick Eagle's own. The nine-foot-long, red and blue beaded belt of the Miami nation was across his left shoulder and wrapped with three turns around his left arm. When he came in, the two visiting chiefs stirred a little, then they rose. Rising Owl rose. Many Thunders next, then all others. At last Quick Eagle stood up, and, chin tipped forward some, tugged nervously at the fringe on his shirt. His father looked like a god.

"We are assembled," Blue Heron said. He looked directly at Quick Eagle. "We were eleven. Now we are twelve." —

The keeper of the door came forward. He helped Quick Eagle remove his shirt, then went back to stand at the entrance of the council lodge.

Rising Owl took charge of the meeting. He directed that Quick Eagle put on an apron sewn with five different snake skins and stand barefooted and bare-chested by the fire. Rising Owl lit a large ceremonial pipe. It was carved like a snake, the duplicate of the one he had smoked with

Blue Heron. Quick Eagle shot a bewildered glance at his father. Was there significance in his smoking the snake-carved pipe with him before?

The pipe was passed and each member smoked in turn. As a man took his puffs he looked upon Quick Eagle. "I accept this member," each man said. When it was his turn, Many Thunders added, "for he has done a great deed and has proven himself to be of courage, strong will, and determination. I find many good things in his character. He is compassionate, kind, truthful, and has the honor of the nation at heart. He was willing to die in shame in order to set an example. Such men are rare. They cannot be wasted, for the loss is too great."

Quick Eagle was then handed the pipe and instructed to say that he accepted the obligations of the Society. He blew puffs of smoke toward each member.

Rising Owl instructed him. Quick Eagle stood with his hands at his sides, his eyes closed and his face uplifted. Rising Owl took an eagle's wing and brushed it across Quick Eagle's face. As the boy kept his eyes shut, Rising Owl dusted pollen on his lids, and Quick Eagle remained motionless, his head tipped back, his hair hanging free, holding the pollen on his lids, the eagle wing in his hand, his lips gently closed.

"You are young," Rising Owl told him. "Do not let it discourage you. Someday you will be as old as I, and then you shall have the wisdom of experience. But, for now, what wisdom there is among us we will share with you. We will guide and direct you. We will help you. Be with us in this brotherhood, Son of Snake. From this place spring our best men, our finest warriors, our greatest leaders, and nobles."

Once again Rising Owl sprinkled pollen on Quick Eagle's lids and on his face and lips.

Quick Eagle held himself very still.

Then he felt his chest being cut with a knife. Many Thunders held the odd-shaped knife and he cut a long wiggly line that represented a snake in motion. "Snakes are warriors and noble fighters," Many Thunders said. "I would be honored to lead you in battle against our enemies."

Another Snake, a visiting chief, stepped up and dabbed at the blood on Quick Eagle's chest with a cloth. "Remember that when you suffer a wound, a Snake will help you staunch it."

Blue Heron came forward with ashes from the fire. He smeared them on the cut Many Thunders had made until a blue tattoo appeared to match the one on his own chest. "Remember, when you lead other men, your lot is one of example. Not only of courage and resourcefulness, but of wisdom to do what is best for all. If you doubt your course, ask the advice of the Snakes you see here, as I have asked many times, and heed the advice that you think wisest. A man is of two arms, two legs, head and heart and flesh and blood and bone. Live inward, in your heart; you will find many more limbs to serve you, many more strengths to help you. Live inward, grow tall."

A fourth man stepped up to him. "This is our brotherhood. We clasp one another's hand, so that if a member falls into darkness, we can pull him forth. If you are lost, we will not rest until you are found. If you are captured, we will bring you home. If you are killed, we will not forget you."

Rising Owl then brushed the pollen from Quick Eagle's eyes. "From the flower," he said, "the pollen that is fertile. Let your mind flower. See inward. Listen to your heart, but let your mind tell you how to do. You increase us by one. We are glad."

When Quick Eagle opened his eyes, Rising Owl had the red and blue belt in his hands, and he put this over Quick Eagle's shoulder and wrapped it with three turns around his left arm. Then Rising Owl looked squarely at each of the eleven other Snakes, each man in turn.

No one objected.

Not one so much as twitched.

Only then did Quick Eagle realize he had been confirmed as hereditary chieftain. When his father died, he would lead the Miami. These men would help him grow into the place his father now occupied. They had waited until he had done an extraordinary thing before they confirmed him, but now he was surely confirmed and made a Snake at the same time.

Black despair rolled in him like a thunderclap. "But I

am white!" he cried within, to himself. "I am white! Oh, I am white!"

Rising Owl relit the large pipe and handed it to Quick Eagle first. Quick Eagle took the pipe just on the tips of his trembling fingers. He offered the stem end up, down, for earth and sky, and to the four quarters of the world. He held it to the east quarter last and longest, for the east was the source of morning, and the morning was the dawn of life.

He smoked slowly, thoughtfully. Once he lifted his eyes and met those of Blue Heron. He looked away quickly and passed the pipe to the man on his right.

What did Blue Heron's smile mean? Did it mean that he saw Quick Eagle as that lost son he had replaced? What did Blue Heron mean by "live inward"? He had lived inward and found himself a cheat. He remembered Blue Heron saying the Miami could not know why the Master of Life did not return some of the young men who had gone naked before him on the Manhood Testing. He did not himself feel returned. Or, if he had come back, it was as a stranger.

Quick Eagle felt below contempt. He saw himself as a vile thing, crawling into the inheritance of a great nation, an intruder, a thief, a white. A white! Oh, why did they not see it? Didn't they understand? He hated the men he sat among for their mistake. He was glad when Rising Owl took the red and blue belt of chiefhood from him and passed it back to Blue Heron. He was glad when the

ceremony in the council lodge was over. Tomorrow
. . . tomorrow he would leave with the whiteskin. He
had to get away now. He could not be chieftain. What if
the council decided on war with the Mitchi Malsa? He
would be expected to go and help kill his brothers.

That night, in his sleeping robes, he twisted and
turned. Alternately he was cold and hot. He shook as
from fevers. He shivered as from icy winds. He was stifled
and gasped for breath. His head rolled from side to side.
He burned, freezing.

"Son?" Blue Heron loomed over him.

Quick Eagle's eyes opened. He couldn't seem to focus
his eyes. Blue Heron looked like a black stone about to
fall and crush him.

Blue Heron placed a hand on Quick Eagle's forehead.
"Son, you are cold. You are freezing."

"I—I am suffering."

Blue Heron lifted the corner of the sleeping robe. He
was going to slip in and hold Quick Eagle in his arms
until he was warm.

Quick Eagle recoiled. *"Don't you touch me!"* he
screamed. *"Don't you ever touch me again!"*

Blue Heron jerked back.

Black, bitter bile rose in Quick Eagle's throat, gagging
him. Every fiber of his body was taut, rigid from shame.

"Father—" he choked. "Oh, my father, I am sorry." He crawled on his hands and knees to Blue Heron. "Oh, my father. Oh—take me in with you for tonight, as in the old times." He tugged at Blue Heron's robe.

Blue Heron lifted the corner of his sleeping robe. Quick Eagle was drawn into a place he fitted, as surely as the nock of an arrow fits the bowstring. He smelled the faint scent of tobacco which was always in his father's hair. It comforted him. He wept over it. He lay sobbing.

"When you are wounded, I bleed, my son."

"Oh, my father, I am still such a boy. Such a boy."

"Youth is not the happiest time of life, but the youth do not know it."

"Father, I cannot be chieftain. I am not fit."

"There is time for you to decide. Later you will know."

"I am not you, my father."

"I am a man, with faults."

"Father, your only fault is me. Father, before I came you must have been a god."

Blue Heron shook him a little. "Go to sleep, my son. Perhaps the nightmares will never come again, and this is the last time you are a boy. Perhaps you will not need me again and this is my last time to comfort you."

"Father, I do not think the nightmares will ever leave me. Father, when I have them, you come. You come, my father, and hold me like this in your arms. You are strong, Father, and I am weak. I will always be a little boy beside you, Father."

Blue Heron shook him again. "Let me share this nightmare. We can conquer it with a dream."

"I . . . cannot . . . my father. I cannot—"

"Am I in your nightmare, my son?"

"Oh, no, my father."

"Sleep then, my son. Let me hold you until the old gray dog comes around. He will wake us. Then we will go to the river."

Quick Eagle turned a little. He could see Blue Heron's profile against the stars above the smokehole of the lodge. He felt like a small child again. "Tell me stories, my father. Tell me about the great heroes of the past. Tell me in the dark, Father, while I am here with you, in your arms."

Blue Heron's voice began in a tone that was the tranquillity of the night. "Noon Boy," he said, "had a good bow, but he was ashamed of his arrows, for they flew crooked and never hit what he aimed at. Then, one day . . ."

Quick Eagle soon fell asleep, moist eyes and warm open breath against his father's side.

The next morning the British arrived from Detroit. Fall had deepened now. Indian summer was gone, and a crisp wind blew across the brown grass in the long meadow west of camp. On the fringes of the meadow the forest was a deep, rich scarlet, and the thick warm browns of the fallen leaves made a backdrop for the brilliant coats and glittering weapons of the bewigged British officers.

They came from Detroit by canoe, moving across the portage between the headwaters of the Maumee and the curve of the Wabash. They had come by the same trail that Quick Eagle thought to take on the Testing.

Quick Eagle watched the white men with cynical eyes. He saw the brilliant crimson coats and gold swords and white wigs as a show of outward pride that covered an inner weakness. By comparison, Blue Heron stood to meet the British in only his red wool Miami short skirt and moccasins. He had always had little to do with white men's goods. He did not drink their rum or wear their clothing, use their muskets or rifles, preferring a bow and warclub; even his skinning knife was of stone with an edge like blue ice. He wore his hair long, unbraided; it hung down his back like a horsetail. He seemed to fill the space where he stood as completely as the eagle occupies the sky and puts to shame the other birds.

Blue Heron's every gesture was leisurely, exquisite, sure. The crimson coats and bright trappings of the British were a pale display of power and authority beside Blue Heron's unadorned body and easy, effortless grace. And his dark, majestic eyes made him seem more than a man of flesh and blood and bone. One did not have to see the red and blue belt he wore over his left shoulder and around his left arm to know that he was chieftain.

Quick Eagle stood slightly behind him with Many Thunders and two subchiefs. Quick Eagle held the *kukewium* of his father. The kukewium was the battle standard, a ceremonial lance nine feet long from which hung the scalps Blue Heron had taken in battle.

The chiefs sat and the calumet was passed to the British officer who sat with them. A long silence, deep and grave, passed between both sides, and finally Blue Heron spoke as though it had just occurred to him that he would be the one to begin. He lifted his arm; the copper bow guard and the red and blue belt glittered in the sunlight.

"Blue Heron and the nation of Miami welcome the envoy from the king of the island across the Bitter Waters. Our hospitality is our pride. Take feast with us and know that we are your friends. We enjoy trading with the British and are prospered by the price given for our furs."

Through a French interpreter the British officer in command spoke up. He was a lieutenant, and he had a small, wry little mouth which twisted to one side as he spoke. His eyes seemed to blink when they were wide open, and he gave the impression that he saw everything with a good deal of astonishment. His crooked mouth betrayed an expression of restrained disgust.

"My leader, Governor Hamilton, whom you call the Scalp Buyer, and my king, George Rex Third of England, send me to pay warriors to do battle with the whiteskins to the south. These unruly, bad children must be made to do service to their master once more."

Blue Heron fixed his stare on the lieutenant's mouth. He appeared to ponder, a slight smile on his lips. Then, innocently, he asked, "What has this King George done to make his own children angry and unruly?"

When the lieutenant heard this question interpreted he showed—immediately—a good deal of astonishment. He had not come to answer questions but to make arrangements. But he said, "The rebels have denied that King George is their good master and true father."

The interpreter gave the British lieutenant a nervous look. Evidently he was interpreting the words directly but believed he should not be.

"Perhaps," Blue Heron said, "the rebels have found a better father than King George?"

The lieutenant sputtered, but Blue Heron lifted his arm. "You have come asking us to fight children. We are men and warriors. My father was a warrior and I am his son. We understand that unruly children must be disciplined for the good of all. Yet when our own children become mischievous we usually spank them ourselves. Rarely do we ask another man to do it for us. We wonder if King George has lost the power to spank his own children?"

The lieutenant narrowed his eyes and looked at Blue Heron intently. Then he took an attitude of extraordinary patience with Blue Heron. "We English stay in our forts. We English are content to trade with those who come with furs. You do not see the English cutting down the forests. You do not see us changing the land. You do not see us chasing the game away. Was not the land, Kentucky, held aside by all tribes, friends and enemies alike, as a hunting preserve? Yet the Mitchi Malsa, Big Knives, did not honor this sacred hunting ground. They moved in with their cattle and their axes. The Big Knives are evil for Indians. This is plain to see. You know this."

Blue Heron nodded slightly.

The lieutenant smiled, showing triumph.

Blue Heron held out his hand, fingers slightly bent, but with forefinger pointed straight at the Englishman. "You say the Big Knives are the children of King George?"

"That is so."

"Yet you say that also they are bad for Indians. Where did the Big Knives learn to be bad for Indians if not from the father who raised them?"

The Englishman's eyes blazed. His face turned as crimson as his coat. He half arose from his sitting position. "Who do you think you are, you savage!" He bit off the words, then touched the interpreter, signifying that the words should not be spoken in Miami. But the Miami knew English words, and they put their hands on their knives and hatchets.

Blue Heron lifted his arm again. He shook the red and blue belt. "Our hospitality is our pride. We do not like men of little authority coming here and telling us we must war on children because King George is in trouble. We do not like to see those who would be our friends with fear of us in their eyes and disgust for us on their lips. We see a man's soul in his face, and your face is plain to me. We suspect you do not trust us. We do not live close to the white men as do the Shawnee and the Delaware and the Mingo and the Iroquois. We know these tribes fight your battles for the pay that you give and for the promises that you make. We Miami sometimes raid into Kentucky. We enjoy battle. We have always believed ourselves capable of making war at our own discretion. These new people, the Big Knives, who were your children a little while ago, have not hurt us personally. We have seen few of them. We do not wish to be put in a place where, one day, you will come to spank us as unruly bad children and say we must do service to the master, King George. So say I, as chieftain."

Blue Heron smiled at the interpreter. "We have not been attacked, tell him, by any of the Big Knives except in the time when they were King George's sons, wearing his scarlet coats. As, you will remember, in the time of the French and Pontiac."

The French interpreter looked thoughtful, then smiled.

The British lieutenant sat back, stunned. "Sir," he said to Blue Heron, "I shall mention your words to Governor Hamilton. He will wish to speak to you himself. I am certain of it."

"It is always good to speak with intelligent men," Blue Heron told him.

Blue Heron lifted his arm, shook the belt again. "My council has given me charge to say that there will be no war this year. We have taken thought concerning ourselves. We fought the English with the French on our side. We did not win. We fought the English with Pontiac and we did not win. The English were too strong for the French and too strong for us. Now the Big Knives have left the side of King George, their original father, and King George has not been strong enough to bring them home. It causes us to think. One day, perhaps, we will call these people, King George's former sons, our friends. It would be a mistake to fight them before we know where they stand concerning the Indians. We know where the British stand, and the French, but we have not heard from the Big Knives. Perhaps they are very small children and have not learned to speak yet. Even so, they are children King George cannot bring home. We are not going into battle with these fierce infants. So say I, Blue Heron, holder of my nation's belt."

The British officer sighed. Then he reached for a box that his aide carried and took out a gold disk which was attached to a blue and white silk ribbon. "This gold medal is a present from my king to the great chieftain, Blue Heron. My king's image is stamped upon the medal so that the Indian will know his friend, and so King George's warriors will know their brother."

Blue Heron took the medal and held it before his eyes. "A handsome man, this King George," he said. "But it is cold material, this gold. I am not sure that it is wise to have an image drawn upon so cold a metal. To take cold metal from a box and hand it to an Indian does not seem good. It is as if King George himself were cold and wished me to warm his gold with my flesh. No, Englishman, I will not be yoked by an image of your king around my neck. I am my own man. So say I, Blue Heron."

He handed the medal back.

"The Master of Life put the tall buck in the forests, the fish in the rivers, the bird in the sky. He made the earth warm with the sun and called the earth Mother. He said to our fathers, 'Light your campfires on the earth's breast, live, my children, and prosper. Make warm lodges when the eye of winter comes.' This now comes, and soon. We wish to be in our lodges with our families. There will be no war. Our hospitality is our pride. Sit and eat with us. Eat of what the Master of Life has provided. The council is over and the Miami have no more words. So say I, Blue Heron."

Quick Eagle relaxed. He was relieved that the Miami were not going to war against the whites in the south. He would not have been able to take part in the killing of whites at war. What if the Miami attacked a fort, over-powered it, and got inside? What if the terror and the horror of his nightmare was repeated? What if he found himself beside Blue Heron or Many Thunders killing whites? What if there were children, little children? Would he be expected to snatch one up and swing it by the heels until—until—

What if he went wild and started to kill a child? What if the child looked like the little blond girl he held in his arms on the morning of the testing? What would happen then?

What would happen to the little white girl now, with-out the war? Would she remember much—fifteen years from now—of her white blood? Would she remember her true father, her true mother, after fifteen years? Would she still wonder about them? Did she wonder about them now? Who was she, really? Where did she come from, really? Was the one Red Panther killed her father?

Quick Eagle shuddered. He remembered now that the scalp Red Panther had worn on his leggings was blond.

The whiteskin in the prisoner hut was red-haired. Was he her father? Or was it the one who was killed? What did the little white girl think, seeing Red Panther with her father's scalp? Did she know? Did she realize it? Was she aware that her father's scalp was a trophy worn by a Miami warrior in order to impress a Miami maiden? A maiden loved by a white man pretending to be Miami?

"Ah, ah, ah," Quick Eagle gasped. He threw back his head, trying to suck in fresh air to clear his head. He was thinking wild, angry thoughts, and didn't know how to stop them.

Then, throwing back his head, he saw it.

The kukewium.

The thing he was holding in his hand. The battle standard. He had seen it a hundred times in the council lodge, but now, for the first time, he really saw it. He saw the scalps on it and knew them for what they were. He saw two blond scalps, one red, three brown—several black. *Which one was the scalp of his true father?* Was the scalp of his true mother here? That one—*that one*—was it a woman's scalp?

"*Aiee!*" he cried and flung the kukewium from him.

Was Blue Heron *proud* of the scalps? He must be. And was the man who carried him over the walls in the nightmare his true father? Did Blue Heron take his scalp? Was it here, now? Which one? Which one? *Which one?*

"Ah, ah, ah." Quick Eagle doubled over. He was becoming physically sick.

Many Thunders picked up the kukewium and shot him an angry look. "Not good thing . . . drop chieftain's . . . standard," Quick Eagle heard Many Thunders say over the roaring in his head.

Quick Eagle straightened up, tense with anger. "I did not drop it!" he cried. "I threw it down!"

Many Thunders stared at him. "I will put it back in the council lodge."

"Yes," Quick Eagle shouted. "Put it there! Put it there! Put the scalp of your daughter beside it. A battle trophy! Something to show off! You will be a hero! All the maidens will smile!"

Many Thunders started for him, hand outstretched. He caught Quick Eagle by the shoulder and started to say something. But Quick Eagle jerked away from his grasp and strode angrily away. The scalps of his own parents had been in Blue Heron's possession all these years. The thought came to him like a blow. What kind of a man was it—what kind of a man was it who kept the parents' scalps and raised their son!

The anger and despair which filled him could not be soothed by those around him and he ignored the friends who gave him a sympathetic touch or glance. Feather Wind stood on the edge of a group of women, watching him, and he met her look with such a fierce, cold stare that she raised her hand as if to protect herself from a blow and melted back into the crowd. Rising Owl, sitting among the old men who smoked and talked, raised a hand slightly to get Quick Eagle's attention. But Quick Eagle would not acknowledge the gesture of his clansman, and the medicine man dropped his hand as he continued to stare at the unhappy boy.

The feast was on. There were whitefish, deer meat, elk steaks, bear, buffalo hump, berries, papaws, maple syrup, honey in the comb, ash and corn cakes. The British provided tea, ship's bread, something called butter. They had bottles of rum. They had pieces of candy wrapped in paper cubes. An Englishman was laughing at an Indian who was confused about the paper on the candy. When the Englishman laughed, the Indian put the candy, paper and all, in his mouth.

Quick Eagle almost drew his knife on the Englishman for laughing. He wanted to lash out and hurt something. He wanted to destroy something. He wanted to fight—he was ready to kill. He glanced up, fingering his knife, and saw Blue Heron.

Blue Heron was wrestling a heavy-shouldered man named Gray Elk. Gray Elk was always challenging Blue Heron, but the chieftain, agile and quick, almost always won the matches. It never seemed to keep Gray Elk from challenging him again. During any large gathering it was an accepted fact that Gray Elk would wrestle Blue Heron and lose.

Gray Elk suddenly sailed up, then down, landing with a thud.

"Oee!" a man cried. "Gray Elk will never learn. A buffalo does not charge a fox!"

Gray Elk was pretending to be badly hurt. "No, I can beat him. He has broken my back, but I can do it. Let me up."

Blue Heron struck a ready stance.

All the while Quick Eagle continued to push through the crowd around Blue Heron and Gray Elk. The desire to hurt Blue Heron overwhelmed him. He wanted Blue Heron to suffer. He remembered how, on the morning of the testing, Blue Heron gave his hair a sharp, cruel yank.

Quick Eagle suddenly put his head down and charged. He charged with all the fury that was in him. He watched Blue Heron's feet for an abrupt shift. He intended to crash full into the man, and once he was down—once Quick Eagle had him down—

But Blue Heron saw Quick Eagle coming. He let out a yip. He let the boy almost reach him, then, with a quick, side-stepping motion, put his hands down and pushed. Quick Eagle went sliding in the grass on his stomach, rapping his chin on a rock in the meadow. He arose, stunned, his head hammering with pain.

Blue Heron stood with one hand on his hip, laughing at him. "Try again, my son?"

Quick Eagle scowled. He set his jaw and pushed his way through the crowd again. He would get the white man, then he would leave.

"Hai-ha!" somebody behind him yelled. "The fox has a blind buffalo for a son! Quick Eagle is not so quick, I think!"

Quick Eagle turned to cry out that his name was not Quick Eagle. But, turning, he crashed into a man and almost knocked him down. It was an Englishman again, this one a little drunk. The Englishman waved a bottle under Quick Eagle's nose. Quick Eagle knew that the whites tried to get the Indians to like rum, for an Indian who craved it would do almost anything to get more. He would sell his furs too cheaply, sell his children, betray his soul, become a drunken wretch, worthless and useless. But Blue Heron's policemen were annoyingly vigilant. They would let a man get thoroughly drunk, then they would drag him to some tree and lash him out of harm's way. Later Blue Heron would try to persuade the man that drinking rum was evil.

Quick Eagle, in a burst of inspiration, snatched the bottle from the Englishman. He saw a way to hurt Blue Heron. It was even better than a physical hurt. He stalked over the ground, going to the spot where Blue Heron was

114

wrestling another man. Quick Eagle ignored the startled looks of the people around him. One Fire came running up to him, but he pushed One Fire aside.

"Ho, Father," Quick Eagle yelled, waving the bottle at Blue Heron. "Look to your son!"

He watched Blue Heron through narrowed lids. His chest rose and fell as the air he gulped went past his nostrils and into his lungs, scorching hot. He wanted Blue Heron to roar with outrage, slap and discipline him like a child in front of all the people. It would shatter Blue Heron's dignity. It would crack his pride. It would humble the chieftain of the Miami. Then Blue Heron would finally admit that Quick Eagle was not his son. Why didn't Blue Heron just admit it?

Blue Heron, holding his wrestling opponent in a hammerlock, suddenly let the man go. The crowd fell silent, so suddenly that Quick Eagle was aware of water rushing over the rocks at the river bend.

"Howah!" Quick Eagle barked. He did a few wild steps of the war dance. Then he tilted the bottle against his lips and howled like a wildcat and drank the rum.

When he lowered the bottle, Blue Heron merely watched him. He stood with arms folded across his chest, one foot, encased in crimson moccasins that matched Quick Eagle's own, a little ahead of the other. He made no move to stop Quick Eagle, just looked on.

Quick Eagle, faltering, howled again. He lurched around, pretending he was already drunk, and he drank more of the rum. It spilled over his lips and splashed on his chest, running down his body. "Give me the belt!" Quick Eagle demanded, throwing back his head. "Let me shake the belt today. My father shakes it. I share the belt. It is my right. I wish to shake it too!"

Several of the warriors crashed their own rum bottles against rocks and stalked off in disgust. Quick Eagle leered at them, his head beginning to spin, and wiped at the sticky rum on his chest.

His fingers encountered the Snake tattoo.

Suddenly Quick Eagle began to cry. He dropped to his knees and hung his head and let the rum bottle slip from his fingers. Then he stretched out full length on the ground and beat the earth with his fists. The rum made him sick and he lay retching, rolling on his side and back. Nothing of his nightmare was as bad as this. Nothing—he had at last done something to kill the nightmare. He would never have it again. He would have instead the memory of this disgusting thing he had done. He rolled and retched and thrashed his body over the ground.

With grave dignity Blue Heron walked over to Quick Eagle and lifted him in his arms as if he were no heavier than a small child. He strode toward his lodge, glancing neither right nor left, at the men who fell back and made way for him to pass. Quick Eagle, limp in his father's arms, saw Blue Heron's stricken face through a haze of tears.

"Why don't you hate me, Father? I am a second-best thing for you. I make a mockery of your greatness. Father, kill me. Father, kill me. Cast me aside."

Blue Heron carried him into the lodge, laid him down gently on the floorskins, and began stripping off his soiled clothes. Patiently, slowly, Blue Heron washed his son. Then he folded Quick Eagle into the sleeping robes.

Quick Eagle looked up at Blue Heron's face. He wished to be taken, fully, into the magic depths of his father's eyes. But Blue Heron kept his head turned aside and his eyes averted.

"Stroke me, Father," Quick Eagle said, catching Blue Heron's hand. "I have a great need that you stroke my arms once more."

Blue Heron pulled his hand free of Quick Eagle's grip. "Not now," he said.

"Father, the need is very great."

"Later."

"Then kill me, Father. Throw me away. I am a second-best thing for you. I have shamed you. I make you small. Oh, my father, I desire that you kill me now."

"When you are wounded, I bleed."

"I have made you small, Father. I am evil, Father. I am destroying you, Father. I cheat you, Father. Kill me. Kill me now. I do not wish to have life. Father, kill me."

"Sleep. Sleep, my son. In the morning when it is quiet, we will talk. It is time for us to have an important talk, and in the morning—"

"Father—Father, I will never shame you again."

"It is good, my son. Sleep now. Rest."

"I cannot be chieftain, Father. I am not you. Father, stroke me. Stroke my arms, Father. The need is so great."

Blue Heron stroked his arms, downward from the shoulders. "Be yourself, my son. You will be much happier that way."

"Father—" Quick Eagle's head filled with dizziness. All things before his eyes blurred and melted together. His mouth burned. His fingers sought the Snake tattoo on his chest.

"Ae and ae," he said. "I will never hurt you—again—my—father. . . ."

Quick Eagle slept.

And he awoke.

And by morning he was gone.

Eight

Jamison Station

When Quick Eagle stepped from the lodge, he found his
friend One Fire sitting under the meat rack with his chin
on his knees, waiting. It was dark now, but the feast fires
still burned in the meadow west of camp. Quick Eagle
could hear the yells of some warriors who were drunk. He
took a deep breath to clear the rum fumes from his own
brain.

One Fire stood up. He took Quick Eagle by the shoulders and shook him a little. "Come now, friend. Let us go
to the feast. I know a new trick that will make everybody
laugh. We will say we have caught a big, black, three-
legged, meat-eating monster with no eyes and ears, just a
mouth and belly. After we collect a present from the
doubters, we will show them my mother's cookpot."

Quick Eagle frowned and shook his head. "I want only
to get away. I am leaving here, and now."

"Why?" One Fire cried. "Oh, why does it matter to you
that you are white? It matters to no other. Where is the
sin in it? There is no sin."

"I do not want my father to have to tell me in the
morning that I am not his son."

"You *are* his son!"

"I have made my father small before all the people. I have spit in his face. I have betrayed the Snakes. I am ashamed of the white blood in me, for it has led me to break many trusts. I am without honor. I have lived inward and seen my heart, which is evil. I cannot look the people in the face again. You cannot wash out the white that is in me. You have seen. White blood is hated by the Indians. Blue Heron should hate the whites. He should fight them as he fought them before, with Pontiac. Perhaps I have robbed my father of his right to hate and his will to fight."

"Blue Heron does what the council wants, and the council is the people!" One Fire said.

Quick Eagle shook his head again. "What Blue Heron wants, the council will do. He is stronger than the council, stronger than the people. The British are right. The Mitchi Malsa are not honorable; they settled in Kentucky and did not honor the sacred hunting lands. Soon they will want more lands, as the British say. The Mitchi Malsa are a people of the ax, and one day, if they win this war, they will come here to clear this land. If Blue Heron hates whites again, he will hate me and he will fight. I cannot fight with him. I could not kill whites. And if I wear the belt after him, how could I lead the nation against my own? No. I am going. It is best." He turned away.

One Fire caught his arm. "Feather Wind—"

"She cannot live in my cave with me. She knows this. She has seen while I stood with the rum bottle in my hand and spit on everybody." Quick Eagle turned his eyes on One Fire. "I am going to take the white prisoners with me. Will you call out an alarm?"

"You cannot take the white prisoners!" One Fire cried.

"I cannot go without them. The white man has promised to help me find my relations, if they are not all dead. He will not leave without the white girl. And I do not want the white girl to stay. She will be hurt. She will suffer, later, as I have suffered." Quick Eagle started toward the prisoner's hut. If the alarm was raised, he would pretend to fight, and he would die as he should have died in the circle.

One Fire stood with eyes downcast. Then he caught Quick Eagle by the shoulder. "Wait. Wait," he said. "We have exchanged blood, you and I, and I must help my brother. I will get the white man and the girl for you. It will be easy for me. You get a canoe and wait where the old oak tree is, by the river bank."

Quick Eagle was surprised at One Fire's sudden change of heart. But it would be easier for him to pretend to relieve the guard at the prisoner's hut, and the white girl would come quietly with One Fire after he rolled his eyes and made her laugh.

After Quick Eagle found his own canoe, he went back

to his lodge for his bow and sleeping robes and for food. Again he looked at the feast fires, hoping to catch one last glimpse of his mother and Blue Heron, but he never saw them. He knew they were leaving him alone intentionally, thinking he was asleep in the lodge.

Quick Eagle's fingertips brushed the poles of the meat rack as he moved away. He would never again hear the old gray dog jumping for the meat. There would not be special treats for him in his mother's cookpot in the mornings after this. His father would not stroke his arms in love and respect and kinship. The old gray dog that lived under the council lodge was like a ghost of the past and a ghost of the future, coming and going, going and coming, the hunger always unsatisfied. Quick Eagle took two pieces of meat from the rack and left it on the ground for the dog, then went to his canoe.

Soon One Fire appeared with the white man. The little girl was asleep in One Fire's arms. "You'll never regret this, boy," the white man said.

Quick Eagle knelt in the stern of the canoe. The white man got in at the bow, and One Fire placed the girl on Quick Eagle's sleeping robes, covering her with one of them.

Quick Eagle looked up at One Fire. "I will not forget you. My heart will always hold some of your blood. And my veins."

One Fire said, "Sometimes I must think of my chieftain. He is my father a little, too. He, too, has his heart, and although he tried to give it all away, he could not."

"What he gave," Quick Eagle said, "I took selfishly, in greed. I will rob no more from him. No more." He dug his paddle into the current. He felt One Fire's fingers on his arm, sliding off his hand, trailing away. One Fire was gone.

Quick Eagle looked back. He could barely make out the round top of his father's lodge. His eyes hardened. He hardened his heart. He thumped the side of the canoe, letting the white man know to work harder, faster, with his paddle. "You are still a slave," Quick Eagle said in Miami. "I am here, behind you with a knife." He thumped the canoe again.

Before daylight he abandoned the canoe to the current of the Wabash and they began the journey overland. If he was followed by Many Thunders or Blue Heron, they would expect him to use the canoe all the way to Vincennes. But Quick Eagle intended going to the lodge of the white man. He wished to be sure the white girl was returned to her true parents. Beyond that, he had not thought.

The lodge of the white girl, said the man—whose name, Quick Eagle learned, was Harmon Briscoe,—called Harm by his friends—was beyond the Falls of the Ohio. Quick Eagle knew the Falls, the only rapids on the Ohio, near the spot where the Miami made canoe caches and sometimes crossed when going on a raid in Kentucky. Quick Eagle had once entertained the notion of making such a raid, and he learned from the seasoned warriors who knew the way which landmarks to follow.

Harm Briscoe had promised to help Quick Eagle find any relatives he might have. He said the girl's name was Jane Sample and that she was the daughter of Matthew Sample, a friend. Matt had gone east, Harm said, with a great chief of the Mitchi Malsa, somebody called George Rogers Clark. Quick Eagle was happy that Jane Sample was not alone in this world like himself, and it comforted him to think he could return her to her true father.

"What it mean, Jane Sample?" he asked Harmon Briscoe on the second night of the overland trip.

"It don't have any meaning," Harm said. "It's just a name."

Quick Eagle was skinning a brace of rabbits he had taken with the bow. Jane was asleep, wrapped in a robe near the low, smokeless fire Quick Eagle had built. "What my white name?" he wanted to know.

Harm rubbed his bristling red beard with his huge hand. "Wal, that's hard to say. Don't you remember nothing about white folks? Nothing at all?"

Quick Eagle shook his head. "I forgot," he said. "You give me a good name. You make it mean something."

"How about John?" Harm offered. "It was the name of my son who died of the smallpox in sixty-nine. He was the reason I headed west, I reckon, sorta in order to forget him dying—and his ma with him o' course. You can be called John. John Briscoe. It ain't much of a name, I guess, but I'd be right proud if you'd use it. John. John Briscoe."

"What does this mean?"

"Means 'Good Friend.' "

Quick Eagle grunted, pointing at Harm with the knife he was using to cut the rabbit meat. "Maybe your people hang up Good Friend by the neck until he is dead? Maybe they think Good Friend is one who killed the blond white man and steal Jane Sample?"

Harm shook his head. "Wasn't you that done it. They'll greet you like a hero. Saving little Jane for Matt and his wife, doing for me what you did. And when they hear the big news—I mean, that we don't have to expect trouble from the Miami—"

"How you know that?"

Harm chuckled. "I got a look at that British lieutenant's face. And I picked up a couple of Injun words, just like you're picking up white words. Easy, ain't it, learning white man's talk?"

Quick Eagle gave Harm a sour look. "You make fun of way I talk!"

"Lord, boy—er—John," Harm cried. "I ain't making fun. I'm just trying to prove to you you're white. If it's easy for you to learn English, then you might be remembering. And if you're remembering, then you might think about something that we can go on later, when we start to look for your folks."

"Maybe white people hang me up by neck for being the *friend* of the Indian that killed other white man." Quick Eagle turned the knife over and over in his hands. "Maybe white Mitchi Malsa Kaintuck blame all Indians for what one Indian does."

Harm rubbed the back of his neck and spat into the fire. "Don't you *want* to find out if you got kin back in the Colonies? Maybe if you're among whites for a while things will start to come back to you. You say you think you were carried off after Venango? Well, anyone finding a body a few miles from Venango would remember it, wouldn't they? And if they knowed him, why then they'd maybe know who the child was that he was running away *with*—you—wouldn't they. It's something we can go on. You got to trust me, boy—er—John. You do, don't you —trust me?"

Quick Eagle finally nodded. Then he spitted one of the rabbits on a green stick and started roasting it over the fire. "One thing, Harm, if I come with you. One thing— important."

"All right. All right. Anything you say."

Quick Eagle turned the knife in his hands again, letting Harm Briscoe see the sharp edge. "Harm, if they want to hang me, you got to cut my throat first. The soul comes from the mouth and cannot get out and go to the

Master of Life if the neck is choked. Harm—you got to cut my throat." He tossed the knife to the Kentuckian. "You promise, Harm."

Harm swallowed hard. "All right," he said. "All right, I promise. If it comes right down to it—which it won't, mind you—then I'll cut your throat."

"Good, Harm. You give me your son's name. It is a good name. But I don't want to be your son, Harm. Don't you try to love me, Harm. You stay away from me. Just cut my throat. You promised."

Harm sat there, holding the knife, staring at the boy. Finally he nodded.

"Good. Now soon we eat."

"Don't want nothin'," Harm said.

"Must eat!" Quick Eagle cried. "We have a long way to go!"

"Ain't hungry," Harm said.

Quick Eagle grunted. White men, he decided, were a little strange. They gave you their name, then wouldn't eat with you.

At the sight of the Jamison Station walls, Quick Eagle felt a moment of panic. It was a fort, like the fort in his nightmare, and he didn't want to go close to it. Harm went ahead, shouting and signaling, calling out his name.

Then the Kentuckians fired off a volley and shrieked a welcome. The gates swung open and the homespun-clad men flooded out, engulfing Harmon Briscoe. They pounded him on the back, laughed and whooped. Harm talked earnestly to them, waving his arms about, motioning for Quick Eagle to come on.

Quick Eagle stepped from behind a tree. He carried Jane Sample in his arms. He had carried her most of the way from Blue Heron's village, overland, across the Ohio, and overland again, to this place of looming log walls and shouting men.

He approached the whites slowly, straight as a water reed. Quick Eagle was a striking figure of young manhood, with slim fine muscles, arresting features, straight back and wide shoulders. His every gesture was, like Blue Heron's, leisurely, eloquent, sure. As he handed Jane Sample over to the outstretched arms of a tearful woman of the settlement he lightly touched the child's face with his fingertips. She wiggled in his arms and pulled one braid, drawing his head down so that she could kiss him on the cheek.

"Thank you, John, for bringing me home," Jane Sample said.

It was hard to reach the hearts of the hard-bitten frontiersmen. But Quick Eagle's graceful manner with the little girl, her kissing him, his smile, caused every man there to rub under his nose and spit carefully to one side.

128

Nine

The Finger

Quick Eagle began living in Hannah Sample's cabin.
Jane's mother took him in gladly, in gratitude for having
her daughter returned. Harm Briscoe did the heavy work
for the Samples while Matt was away, but Quick Eagle
did not see much of him except in the morning and at
night. The Mitchi Malsa lived in the fort and went out
from there to clear land, raise cabins, and dig wells. But
two days after Quick Eagle came, there was a heavy
snowfall and work outside the stockade was abandoned
until spring.

Quick Eagle went out to watch the men chop firewood
and the women and children shovel snow to keep the
passages of the stockade clear, piling the snow up outside
the walls. He looked on, smiling, but would not touch an
ax or do any work himself. He stayed close to Harm.

The night of the third day came, and the Mitchi Malsa
held a celebration. They whooped and hollered, listened
to screeching music from what Harm said was a fiddle,
drank cider and rum, and stomped around on the board

floors in all sorts of wild approximations of what Quick Eagle considered a war dance.

Quick Eagle was overawed that the Mitchi Malsa were so coarse a people, and liked them in spite of it. They cursed, laughed, shouted, sang, stuffed big wads of raw tobacco in their mouths, hawked and spat and looked importantly at the sky and said "Wal" a lot. Their cabins inside the fort were stuffy, their bodies gave off odors of the unwashed, they had unkempt, matted hair and dirty hands and yellow teeth, and their garments, for the most part, were stiff with grime.

They were a crude people, very new at being away from the side of King George, and very much like the children the British said they were, Quick Eagle thought. He did not see many signs of dignity and no traces whatever of leadership, and he could not decide whether they had a council of wise men anywhere to help them with their affairs. But probably not, since they were wild, strong children who did not seem to care in the least what their warriors were doing in the East, against King George, although each man spoke loudly about "freedom" and what he would do if he saw a "Redcoat" in this "neck" of the woods.

The women came often and spoke to Quick Eagle, trying to help him remember his white childhood. The youths came, to touch his bow and arrows, wanting to see his Snake tattoo and get him to help make them one just like it on them. They wanted to see him wear feathers and dance. They asked him to paint his face, and people who happened to touch him or shake his hand would sometimes wipe their hands, the women on their skirts and the men on the seat of their pants. This habit disgusted Quick Eagle. It was as if they thought to wipe him off.

In Hannah Sample's small cabin inside the fort he was happier. Matt Sample's wife, the fourth morning, cut his hair and sewed together white man's clothing made from some kind of itching cloth. He was too well brought up not to accept their hospitality, but when his breechclout and leggings and braids went into the fire, he moaned.

Hannah Sample admired the beadwork on the moccasins he wore.

"They are like my father's," he told her. "Only now I cannot wear them. I could never wear the moccasins of my father," he said. "They were too large. Burn them."

Hannah Sample did not burn them. She put them in a large wooden chest, and from the same chest took out a book. "Have patience, John," she told him. "Put your trust in God. In the spring the men will be going to the East for powder and supplies and seed corn and news. One of them will put a notice about you in the weeklies. In God's good time news of your family will reach us. You'll see. And if there is nobody of your own, why, we'd be proud to have you stay with us. Will you kneel and pray with me? It's Sunday."

"Sunday?"

"The Lord's day, John."

"Is—is—God—"

"God. Say it, John."

"God. Is God like the Master of Life?"

Hannah Sample smiled. "He's the same, John. God has different names, but He is the same God everywhere. Do you know how to pray, John?"

"Sometimes I would pray. I did not kneel."

"It is better to kneel, John."

"When I pray, it is with a pipe. I blow smoke to Earth and Sky and to the Four Quarters of the World. The smoke takes my words up to places I cannot go myself. When I die, I will be in a place where the arrows are sunbeams and the deer do not really die. Do you believe this?"

"Yes, John. Where the arrows are sunbeams."

"You kneel," he said to Hannah Sample. "I will get a pipe. Harm has a pipe I can use, maybe."

"All right, John."

Quick Eagle glanced around the cabin, saw Jane Sample at the table playing with a doll. "She will pray too?"

"Yes, John."

Quick Eagle smiled. "I am glad you have God. I was afraid for the Mitchi Malsa. But they will be all right if they have God."

Quick Eagle went for Harm's pipe, but before he

reached the place where it was kept, the alarm bell of Jamison Station sounded and he rushed outside.

The Kentuckians were running for the shelves on the walls to peer out of the loopholes. Women began to cry. Hannah Sample behind him screamed and grabbed up little Jane. Men came to lead her to the powder magazine. Guns rattled and kegs of bullets and black powder were hauled to the walls. The Kentuckians ran every which way, shouting a jumble of words, yelling at one another, cursing. It was easy to see they needed a leader, a chieftain, to speak clear words for all.

It was some time before Quick Eagle realized that Jamison Station was under attack. He went to the walls and found Harm Briscoe. "What is it, Harm?"

Harm Briscoe's jaw was grim. He pointed.

In the fresh snow outside the fort stood the Miami nation, painted for war.

The Indians stood in a ring around the fort, almost four hundred warriors, just out of rifle range, and there was a British redcoat among them. As he watched, three men stepped from the ring. One was the British officer Blue Heron had upbraided only a few days ago. The other was Many Thunders, and the third man was Blue Heron.

Blue Heron was hard to recognize. He was shaved to a

scalp lock, a high center ridge of hair bristling with porcupine quills dyed red. His face was streaked with diagonal stripes of black and white. His right arm was scarlet to the elbow, his killing arm. Four heron plumes, dyed blue, dangled from a braid-of-three scalp lock that hung between his shoulders. The copper wristguard glimmered on his bow arm. He carried the kukewium forward and planted the spear end in the ground. He raised his scarlet arm and made a sweeping motion toward the circle of his warriors around him.

"Ow, ow, ow!" the Miami cried. They beat their rifles and muskets and tomahawks and knives together until the clatter reached a tremendous volume. Then, on Blue Heron's signal, the clatter ceased and there was no sound at all. The silence washed over Jamison Station, and the Kentuckians looked at one another in wonder.

Quick Eagle hugged the log wall, peering out through a loophole. Blue Heron looked magnificent. Splendid. Like a god. He had never before seen his father dressed and painted for battle. The sight of him sent thrills through Quick Eagle. His blood pounded at his temples and at his wrists. He was enraptured by the scene.

He hardly heard the words the British officer was shouting. His eye stayed on Blue Heron, his mind raced with thoughts. The council had decided against war. Why was Blue Heron here?

Harm Briscoe tugged at Quick Eagle's arm. "He wants

to know what I've done with your body! He thinks I killed you! The Britisher said if I'm not handed over to them immediately, they won't stop their attack until every last one of us is upside down over a fire!"

"My *body!*" Quick Eagle cried. "He thinks I am *dead?*"

Harm shook Quick Eagle roughly as the other Kentuckians crowded around with dark looks for the boy. "Look here," Harm roared. "This ain't some kind of a trick, is it? How'd he know where I was? You been signaling him or something?"

Quick Eagle drew back in shock. "How would I signal him? I did not even know he was here until now!"

Harm looked as though he might strike Quick Eagle. "How'd he know where to come? He's come for you, ain't he?"

"He just guessed! He knows you were captured near this place. Maybe his scouts saw you walking on the walls today or yesterday. Maybe he has scouts in all places where there are white forts. He's not dumb! He knows how to do!"

Tod Jamison, in charge of the station, pushed forward. "Listen here, Briscoe," he said. "Is that Injun the one who adopted this boy? Is that what he's come for?"

"He thinks John is dead!"

"Throw the whelp out of the fort!" a Kentuckian cried. "That's all the Injuns want, this red-hide whelp! I never thought we should of took him in in the first place!"

Jamison cursed. "You know John's white!"

"*White?* Fifteen—sixteen years with Injuns and you say he's *white?* He's a red-hide whelp and there ain't no two ways about it!"

Jamison ran his hands over his face. "Heaven help us. Did you count them? There's four hundred Injuns out there and in a mean mood. I've got thirty-six men in this fort! I knew we should have pulled back to Harrodsburg like George Clark advised. We should've pulled back when Harm returned!"

"Wal, we ain't pulled back. And them Injuns ain't gonna wait forever. They got British—maybe a cannon in the woods. We got to do something, Jamison, and quick!"

"Grab the boy," said Jamison. "Raise him up, over the top of the wall so the Injun can have a good look at him. Maybe if he sees the boy ain't dead it'll be to our advantage."

Four men grabbed Quick Eagle and lifted him. Quick Eagle let them. He helped, holding on to the tops of the logs, and when he was high enough, he waved.

"Look at him!" somebody yelled. "The hellion!"

The instant Quick Eagle's head and shoulders had appeared above the walls, the Miami raised the war whoop. They cupped their hands over their mouths and joined their voices in a cry that rolled across the woods. "*Ow-ow-ohhhhh! Ow-owhhhhhh!*" They crashed their steel weapons together. Blue Heron took a step forward, passing the imbedded kukewium which must have marked the limit of a rifle's range. He signaled for silence, then shook his fist and cried out angrily.

The Kentuckians let Quick Eagle drop out of sight of the Indians. "What'd he say?" Harm demanded.

"He says let me go. If you let me go, he no kill everybody, no torture. If you do not let me go, or if you kill me, he will do the worst things. Women, children, men—he will turn the warriors loose. You burn. And before you burn, the worst things. He says the snow you have piled up outside the walls will let his warriors jump easily into the fort. He says let me go. He says he will wait while the British officer counts to five hundred. Then he comes."

Tod Jamison went to the corner of the wall and climbed up on a bullet keg to look at the Indians outside. He struck the logs with his fist. "Dear God," he said. "The piled-up snow."

"Shoot the red-hide and fight!" a man yelled. "He can't take us all alive."

Jamison whirled. "He'll take some! If he takes just one it's too many, ain't it? Just one is too many, ain't it?"

Harm shouted, "And John is one of us! I say, defend him the same as we would anybody else."

Jamison struck his forehead with his fist. "Harm, it ain't the same. It just ain't. This boy is Injun."

"That's right!" a man cried. "It ain't the same. That

137

kid brought them Injuns here one way or another and he's to blame, nobody else. Harm told us them Injuns wanted peace. Now they're here and that kid brung 'em. Shoot him and fight until we have to light the charges in the powder house and blow up our women and kids. Them's facts! What's all the argument about?"

Somebody raised a gun at Quick Eagle.

Harm knocked it aside. "Don't be a fool. That bunch can take us whether John's alive or not. We've only got one chance—let this boy go. That's our only hope."

Quick Eagle glanced at the powder house and thought of Jane and Hannah Sample. "Harm," he said. "Harm—I have been here before. In a place like this, long ago. I dreamed about how it was. Harm—Harm you do not know how—how—" He motioned with his arm. "It will be a nightmare, Harm. Harm, your people are good to me, but your people are not my people anymore. Your people and my people are not the same. I will ask my father not to fight with you. Maybe he will be satisfied with killing me."

"Kill you!" Harm said. "Why would he want to kill you?"

"He wants to see my body. He wants to kill me because I betray him. I am a thief. I stole you and Jane and he has come to punish me—see my body. It is good that he came. I am proud."

Harm's mouth dropped open. "Proud! What—what

138

in—what have they done to you, boy? Blast it! Jamison. We can't let them kill John. No telling how they would do it. They might torture him, right out there in plain sight."

Jamison looked at Quick Eagle. "You mean you *want* to go out there and try to help us by giving up your own life?"

"It would help me more than you," Quick Eagle told him. "It is the only way I can feel honorable again. It is like—the circle. You do not know that, but it is something you must do, because it is the only way for honor, Harm. I do not want my nightmare here. You make them let me go."

A heavy silence fell over the men in Jamison Station. All eyes turned to Quick Eagle, then looked away from him. "Aw," a Kentuckian finally spoke up. "Give the kid a gun and let's fight like men."

Tod Jamison touched Quick Eagle's arm. "You mean you'd let them kill you in the hopes they'd go away?"

"Not sure they would go away. Maybe they would. But I am not sure."

Harmon Briscoe said, "Come on, lad. I'll show you how to load and fire a rifle gun."

"I will not kill Indians!" Quick Eagle cried.

"Boy! Boy! We can't hand you over like a sacrifice!" Tod Jamison yelled at him.

Quick Eagle had had enough. It was clear to him that both Indians and whites would die because of him. With a sudden motion he leaped and got a handhold on the stockade pickets, swung up and over and dropped in the snow below.

The Miami howled again. *"Ow-ow-ohhhhhh!"*

Quick Eagle stood up and walked toward Blue Heron. He dimly heard Tod Jamison telling the Kentuckians not to shoot. He heard Harm Briscoe cursing.

Quick Eagle stopped before Blue Heron. "I am here," he said. "Ae and ae. I have come."

There was the merest twitching of Blue Heron's eyelids under the black and white striped paint. His mouth and nose and expression were lost in the design. Quick Eagle marveled at the change war paint made in Blue Heron. He glanced down at Blue Heron's red-painted killing arm.

"I am here," he said. "I must take what comes. I cannot weep." Quick Eagle lowered his chin to his chest, head bowed. "Do with me as you will. I am ready."

Blue Heron's great hand came out, touching the side of Quick Eagle's head where the braids had been shorn. And a moan escaped the chieftain of the Miami. "Ahh," he said, low. "Ahh." And his hands moved again, and he stroked Quick Eagle's arms downward, from the shoulders to the elbows, in love.

"Ow-oh-ohhhhh!" The Miami in the ring howled. "We have found the future chieftain! *Ow-ow-ohhhhh!*"

Quick Eagle looked up in surprise. It came to him then

that all was forgiven. He realized for the first time why his people were here. They called him "chieftain." They called him chieftain and forgave him his behavior at the council, his leaving with the white captives—all. They forgave him all.

"O, my father," he said. "You have come for me, your son?"

"I have come. Did you not think I would?"

Quick Eagle embraced him. His lips moved in voiceless wonder. He stroked his father's arms. "O my father. You are my father. There was no other before you. I love you dearly. Take me home and teach me again. Let us leave this place in peace. We are finished here."

Blue Heron held him close. He smiled at his son. "Paint, O my warrior, for battle. We will roll over them together, you and I. I will make the whiteskin who took you from me sorry. I will draw his soul from him piece by piece."

"Father!" Quick Eagle cried. "The white man did not take me! *I took him!*"

Blue Heron started. "Nay—nay, son. One Fire said the white man escaped and took you for his hostage. I thought to find your body and give it proper burial; that the Master of Life need not stoop for your soul. But—but I found you alive!"

Quick Eagle shuddered. *One Fire had lied to save Blue Heron's feelings and Quick Eagle's honor!*

One Fire had lied! Blue Heron had come to get back a captive son, according to his oath as an Elk clansman and a Snake—not to capture a runaway!

"Father, it is not true! One Fire lied to protect me. He could not believe you would understand why I left. Father! *One Fire lied!*"

Blue Heron stepped back from Quick Eagle. He pointed at the walls of the fort with his scarlet-painted arm. "Did they throw you over that wall? Or did you jump?"

"I jumped, Father! I jumped!"

Blue Heron still pointed. "Did you think to buy me off with your love? Did you think to trade upon my love for you in order to save the whiteskins' lives? Do you think you have goods buried in my heart that you may dig out any time you please? Do you think my heart is for sale? Do you think that you are worth more to me than my honor or my nation?"

Blue Heron leaned toward Quick Eagle with an awful intensity. The chieftain restrained his twitching, scarlet-painted killing arm with his left hand. His voice was low, deadly. "I have denied the advice of my council for you. I would make war and have men die in your name. I came for my son because I loved him more than life. I loved that son more than what comes after life. Now you have killed my son. You have killed him here and now, and he is dead."

Blue Heron jerked out his knife. Quickly, before anyone could move, he slashed around the joint of his index finger and then broke the finger off, throwing it at Quick Eagle's feet. "Whites expect payment for what they do. You are paid. This is all you shall have from me. It is finished."

Blue Heron turned on his heel and walked away. The British officer rushed toward him and grasped his arm, urging him to attack the fort. But Blue Heron swung his scarlet arm without a backward glance and knocked the lieutenant sprawling in the snow.

Quick Eagle began to run after him. "Father!" he cried.

But Many Thunders blocked his path. "Be content we do not draw your dog's blood from you. You have shattered him, he that gave you only love. The thing that crawls beneath your skin sickens me. Come not north, whiteskin, for it will be the sacred duty of every Miami man to kill you on sight. So say I, Many Thunders."

He pushed Quick Eagle aside and jerked Blue Heron's battle standard free. He looked steadily, long and hard, at the walls of Jamison Station. He studied the rifles on those walls. His war paint glistened, then an eyelid drooped and he held up his arm to signal. "Howah!" Many Thunders barked and swept with his arm—swept north.

The Miami turned away into the snow-covered forest without a further sound.

There was only the bloody finger in the snow, pointing.

Part Two

WHITE HAWTHORN ROSES

1778

Ten

Matt Sample

John Briscoe was halfway down the road to his lean-to when he heard the hoofbeats. His first inclination was to duck into the underbrush, then he smiled to himself and cast the rifle-gun into the crook of his left arm and stood waiting in the road.

When the roan mare came around the bend, he recognized it as one belonging to Tod Jamison. A tall Kentucky hunter was in the saddle, a raw-boned, blond man holding a long rifle across the horse's withers. The rider reined in, showing surprise, and John caught the horse's bridle and grinned.

John guessed it was Matt Sample. For the past few weeks Harm had been expecting Sample's return at any moment, and when John had last seen little Jane she could talk of nothing but her father. Sample had been east, to a place called Fort Pitt at the forks of the Ohio, recruiting an army under George Rogers Clark. Sample had left with Clark last fall. It was now June of 1778 and the white roses were budding on the hawthorn.

Matt Sample grinned down at John and offered his

hand. "Well," he said, "you got a face I ought to know but don't. You new in this part of Kentucky? I'm Matt Sample. My land is down the road a piece."

"Yes, I know," John replied. "My name is John Briscoe."

At that Matt raised his eyebrows. "Kin to Harmon Briscoe?"

"In a way. He's at your farm putting in a crop and girdling trees. He's been at it since early this spring. I help him around your cabin. He'll be glad to see you. Everyone is well."

Sample nodded. "So Tod Jamison told me. He wanted to tell me a lot else, but I got away from there quick as I could. I've been gone most a year. You going to my place? The horse'll pack double."

John shook his head. "No"—he motioned vaguely—"I live over there."

Sample looked. "Nothing over that way but woods," he said. He rubbed his jaw, squinting at John. "Come to think of it," he said, "Jamison did mention something about a hunter who kept the watch for Indians. I had him pictured as sorta—sorta older."

"It is what I do—best," John said. "Look for Indians."

"Well, be careful. The British have hundreds of them roaming these woods."

"I'll be careful," John Briscoe told Matt. "If I see any, I'll give your people warning."

Matt Sample nodded and galloped off. John watched him go, then turned toward his meadow. He lived alone, two miles from Jamison Station. He was called a "meat hunter" for the stockade. Few whites ventured out of sight of the walls, and by hunting meat, John earned his powder and shot, salt and gear, and he did some trapping now and then. He went as far north as the Ohio, looking for signs of hostiles.

It was not true, as Matt suggested, that hundreds of British-inspired Indians roamed these woods. It was true that small war parties had passed between the forts, cabins, and clearings in Kentucky, but John had never come across signs of more than a dozen or so at a time. Raiders out for loot or glory—not hundreds of warriors at all. John had learned that where he saw signs of one Indian, the settler was liable to imagine he heard six hundred or a thousand. Fear was what the white settler saw, and worry was how he counted. The entire Shawnee nation was not able to put out a force of four hundred braves, and the Shawnee were about the only close-by tribe who would make war on the Mitchi Malsa. Except, as with the Miami, for independent glory hunters like Red Panther, or child stealers like Many Thunders.

John had never forgotten how Many Thunders looked at Jamison Station after Blue Heron stalked off. He knew now that Many Thunders had been thinking of little Jane, whom he had come to think of as his daughter.

Probably because of little Jane, Many Thunders decided not to attack the fort. She would surely have been killed.

The lean-to John had built was tight and comfortable. He'd made it on the design of a Miami lodge, bending saplings to a common center, then covering them with sheets of bark. Grass from the meadow made his floor thick and warm, and he slept by a hearth in the center of the lodge, under a deerskin.

He rejected the idea of staying always with the whites, and there were whites who wanted it that way. He expected he would become, eventually, one of those shaggy old men who came from "yonder" headed for "nowheres" —"free trappers" they called themselves. Actually they were failures, running from duty or obligations or the law in the East. The settlers were more permanent, but they were restless and would move on west one day—always westward. Movers, Harm called them, people who couldn't make a go of it in the East, and people persuaded by the town builders, like Boone and Jamison and Bryant and Harrod, to come West, where the land was cheap. Such a person could easily see a dozen Indians where there were none, and hate what he feared or couldn't understand.

The white man was curious. He chopped at everything, burned off and looted the earth. He tried to make the forest do things it could not do. He raised homes that looked strong but were airless, cheerless, smoky, and harbored disease and filth. Most of the children born in these cabins were sickly, and the chance of surviving birth was only one in ten. The white settler rarely bathed and had a peculiar, sweet-sour odor that John almost couldn't stand.

The white man cursed the weather, the earth, the forest, and blamed himself for coming here—west. He was fearful, jealous, grim, suspicious of his neighbors; but he kept coming. The white man lived wretchedly on the frontier, but more of his kind kept coming and endured the hardships, suffered and died, and more came. They hated the wilderness, but they knelt on the Lord's day and prayed to the sky, and they came away from their prayers confident that "tomorrow will be better."

The Indian let the forest absorb him, and was absorbed by it. The Indian selected a beautiful place by a stream for his home, where there would be berries and wild vegetables and good hunting, natural shelter from the winds, natural mounds and gullies for defense. When he built his lodge, he judged the size of the family he would shelter, selected just enough peeled sapling poles and slipped just enough bark from the trees to make his walls. The tree did not die but produced forever what the Indian would need.

The Indian wasted no food, cutting out the best parts and throwing the rest away or letting it spoil as did the white man. He made use of the animals he killed; hoofs and hide, fur and sinew. Thus he was made strong as the sinew of the Master of Life who made him naked and clothed him and fed him and made him happy under the sun.

Now that Quick Eagle, alias John Briscoe, was alone and was neither a white man nor an Indian, he had learned these lessons by himself.

Yet he could have respect and awe for white men. One thing they did pleased him very much: When there was a stream that they crossed often, the whites built a bridge.

Often John went out of his way to cross on the little bridge above Jamison Station, and he always paused there on the bridge, remembering how on his Manhood Testing he had paused on a log with his pack of furs. A man might cross a stream without a thought, but it was a good man who built a dry passage for others who followed behind; others the bridge builder would never see or know—and maybe even enemies.

Yes, it took a very good man. John believed that bridges were the final triumph of the white man's culture. The log in the forest had been a bridge, dropped into place by the Master of Life, that Quick Eagle might easily cross into manhood. But the restless white in Quick Eagle caused him to reject that easy crossing, just as he had rejected the unselfish love of Blue Heron and his nation of people.

Now there was only the white man's bridge. Even if storms should destroy this bridge, John knew people would always remember where it had stood and, using materials the storm did not destroy or carry away, build another. A bridge was a good thing. It covered a gap. But to stand on a bridge, unable to reach either shore, able only to look at the waters and time rushing past, was a terrible thing. North shore, Indian; south shore, white— but John Briscoe stood in the middle, alone, touching neither side.

He knew back in the Indian lodge where the silver water tumbled nearby and the coals of many fires glowed and the old gray dog jumped vainly for meat—there his name was never mentioned. He was dead.

And here, among the white men, he was dying.

And each day he died a little bit more.

At sundown on the day Matt Sample came home, Harm Briscoe came up, riding on Jamison's mare, which, John guessed, he was returning for Matt. Harm swung down, stooped, and entered to sit down heavily on a pile of deerskins next to John. "Matt's home," was all he said.

"Yes," said John. He was kneeling, holding his face to

one side and peering into a mirror while he shaved his chin. His beard was silky, but black and nearly full. "Harm," he said.

"Huh?" Harm started. He had been looking at John closely.

"Harm, sometimes I think I wish the whites had wanted to hang me when I first came. Then my soul would have gone to the Master of Life when you cut my throat."

"Don't talk crazy!" Harm cried.

John shrugged, putting down the knife and feeling his face, looking at it in the mirror. "Maybe there is no soul in me to come out. Maybe the Master of Life knew this all along. Is there not a place the white man has for those with no soul? Is it not called 'hell,' Harm?"

Harm glared at him. "You got soul enough for half the people in Kentucky," he said. "And heart enough for a nation. And maybe, just maybe, God's taking an interest in both right about now."

"Maybe the Master of Life sent me to find out about hell. The Indians do not have this place, and so my father could not explain it to me. If he knew of it, he would have said."

"Now stop that!" Harm yelled. "I—well—I—er . . ." Harm Briscoe got up, went to the doorway and spat, then came back and sat down. "I got something to say," he

154

growled, "and it ain't about hell. It's about heaven, maybe. You got any interest in heaven anymore?"

"Do you also believe it is a place where the arrows are sunbeams and the deer do not really die?"

"That sums it up pretty neat, lad. That's just how it is, I figure. But I been busy lately, thinking about things on earth. You want to hear a story about—something?"

John smiled. "My father, sometimes, would tell me stories. He knew about all the heroes, Harm. All of them."

"Well," said Harm, "I ain't got any like that. This here is one about Matt Sample. You know he's been east, helping George Clark recruit volunteers for an expedition? Well, most of the recruiting was done along the Monongahela River, the forks of the Ohio country. Clark got a lot of misfits, and some pure adventurers, and some mighty good men too. Everything's up to Corn Island near the Falls of the Ohio where you and me and Jane Sample crossed last fall. Remember?"

"Clark will build a bridge there?" John asked.

Harm stared at the boy. "Bridge?"

John shrugged. "It means nothing, Harm. A joke, on me."

"Well, anyway," Harm went on, "there'll be men from Harrodsburg, some from Jamison Station, and one or two over from Boonesboro. And, while I'm thinking of

Boone, you know that Shawnee kid you told me about—what's his name—Tecumtoo?"

"Tecumseh. It means, I Cross Somebody's Path."

"Do it now? Well, anyway, ol' Dan'l Boone got away from them Injuns. Escaped clean away from Black Fish his Injun pa one day. Just like you."

"Just like me," John said. "Does Black Fish have four fingers on one of his hands now?"

Harm cursed. "I come here to talk to you! I don't aim to talk no more, not if you're going to keep bringing that up! I told you, don't talk about it. Just makes it worse!"

"All right, Harm. All right."

"All right, then. Now—now listen. Clark's got almost everything he needs except for one thing. He ain't got a real good Injun interpreter. Want the job?"

"You want me to be a whiteskin warrior, Harm?"

"We aim to fight the British."

"No Indians?"

"Not unless we got to. That's why it'd be a good thing if we had somebody to tell 'em we come peaceful and don't aim to hurt 'em."

John shook his head. "No. I'll stay here."

Harm chewed his lip. "Think you might run into your Injun pa up there, huh? Scared maybe, huh?"

"I might, Harm. It is the duty of the Miami men to kill me. I could not fight back. While they are killing me, you might be hurt."

"Forget it, lad. That's the way things are. But that ain't the only thing I come to say. In fact, I ain't even started to tell you the story yet. Reckon you can stand a real, genuine shock?"

"Shock?"

"John, there's a man at Corn Island with Clark, a sergeant in Helm's company by the name of Daniel Cutchen. Like Daniel Boone, see, only his last name is Cutchen. *Cut-chin!* Mean anything to you? *Cut-chin?*"

John laughed. "It is what you do when you wait until sundown before you shave."

"May be," said Harm, rubbing his face with a huge hand. "But this Cutchen is from the Allegheny country, up around where Fort Venango used to be—"

"Venango?"

"That's right. He joined up when Matt and Clark were recruiting at Fort Pitt, and he and Matt got to be good friends. This Daniel Cutchen carries a locket with the portrait of a pretty Spanish lady in a lace shawl. There's a baby in the lady's arms, but Matt said the lady died soon after it was painted. The baby was brought up by Daniel's sister. She was married to one of the settlers near Fort Venango back in sixty-three, the year Pontiac's braves massacred the fort and left no survivors. Somehow the sister's husband managed to jump over the wall with this child, even though he had arrows and musket balls in him. He was found dead three miles away, though, a few

157

days later. Somebody had wrapped him in a deerskin robe and put him in a tree fork so the wolves wouldn't get him. He wasn't scalped. He died trying to reach Cutchen's cabin, they figure. They never found any trace of the boy—dead or alive. And Daniel—well! he's kind of been looking all these years. That's mainly why he was eager to join Clark and come west. He'd been all through the East. . . ."

Harm raised his voice. "John! He's your real flesh-and-blood father! He's just *got* to be! Wasn't Hannah Sample right when she said 'In God's good time'? Your name's *Cutchen*, lad! *Daniel* Cutchen. Just like your pa."

Corn Island lay a few miles above the Falls of the Ohio. It was a wedge-shaped island, timbered on the west end, sand bar to the east, facing the current. Four flatboats lay against the south bank, bridging the waters in a chain. John, crossing over with Harm and Matt and a file of volunteers, saw that guards were posted near a stack of kegs which smelled awful.

"Buffalo meat," Matt Sample said. "What we eat. It's rotten. All we could get in Fort Pitt." He crinkled up his eyes, pointing ahead with the muzzle of his rifle. "Clark's drilling 'em, companies of forty men. I hope he ain't as particular about his men as he usually is or he'll weed out all but fifteen or twenty. Men don't like drilling much. Besides that, Clark ain't told 'em yet where they're going. Those guards aren't for the meat—they're in case of deserters."

John looked around at the men. It had been raining, but the rain had stopped and he watched a company march through a puddle on the sand bar. "Which one is my father?" he asked.

Matt looked around. "Don't see him. He might be with Clark. They're going to build a blockhouse here, leave most of the meat behind. And some of the sick or hurt. Come on, Daniel—"

John tugged nervously at his buckskins, eyes downcast. He'd made his own leathers—moccasins, shirt, breeches —in the white man's style. "I like the name Harm gave me," he said. "I like John Briscoe. Call me that, please, Matt."

"All right. All right, lad." Matt led the way to a cluster of leather-clad men who squatted on their heels under a keelboat sail stretched between keelboat poles thrust into the ground. One of the men stood up when Matt approached. He seemed very young to be a Big Knife colonel. George Rogers Clark was twenty-four, a tall man with flaming red hair, dressed in smoke-blackened buckskins like his men.

Clark smiled at Matt. "See your family, Sample? They all right?"

"I don't suppose anything else will happen to them that hasn't happened already." Matt jabbed a finger at John and introduced him to Clark as John Daniel Cutchen. He began to talk, starting with the words "captive boy" and ending up with "Sergeant Cutchen's locket."

Clark rubbed his nose with the knuckles of his right hand and looked at John. "Used to live in a lean-to myself. Lived in it maybe five years. Lonesome. Used to squat up there on a hill and watch the settlers building cabins on the land I'd surveyed. Something permanent about a cabin—lean-to gets to leaking now and then and a man who is used to it just don't bother about fixing it. Lonesome. Plenty lonesome. A man needs somewhere to belong. You figuring on joining us, John Cutchen? If you do, you'll have to sign articles of enlistment. But if you run out on what you agree to, you'll be shot." Clark motioned toward the guards by the kegs of meat.

"My father—" John said.

Clark made an angry motion. "It ain't up to your father. I'm asking you."

John looked away. "I do not know."

"When you know," said Clark, "then come and tell me. We can use you as an interpreter, scout, plain soldier. Probably all three. I hope we don't have to fight Indians, but if we do, and if you sign articles of enlistment, you'll fight too. Or you'll be shot. I'll do it myself. What do you say?"

"I have to—think."

"You think then," Clark told him. "Until morning. If you haven't made up your mind by then, get off the island. Sample, Briscoe, that's an order. You heard it."

Matt Sample nodded, and so did Harm.

Clark nodded at them. "Sergeant Cutchen is on the north bank, hunting for fresh meat. He'll be back soon. Sample, you stay here with me. I want to go over something with you. Briscoe, you ain't in this outfit yet. You go sign in now."

"Shore," Harm said, "—er—Colonel—er—sir."

It was dusk when Daniel Cutchen came across to Corn Island from the north bank of the Ohio with a buck deer over the thwarts of his canoe. He was a tall, heavy-shouldered man with a black beard and crow's-feet in the corners of his eyes and a weathered-brown face. His black hair was gray at the temples. Watching him beach the canoe and splash through the shallows as he yelled for men to come for the deer, John studied him, point for point. He could see that they did not look anything alike.

Daniel Cutchen grinned and waved at Matt Sample, who had come away from Clark a while ago. "Family all right, Matt?"

Matt muttered something. "Fine—fine." He hesitated, then poked with his fingers. "This is—uh—somebody special, Daniel. It's—Harmon Briscoe from Jamison Station."

"Oh, sure"—Daniel came up, holding out his hand—

"Matt talked about you. You were looking out after his family while he was east, wasn't you?"

"Tried to," said Harm. "Not much good at it, though," he admitted.

Daniel noticed John for the first time as he shook Harm's hand. "This your boy, Harm?"

"Why?" Harm asked. "Why'd you think he might be?"

"I just wondered. Well—" He looked at John again and smiled. "I've got work to do." He turned away. "Reminds me of somebody, though," he said, half to Matt, half to himself.

Matt caught Daniel Cutchen by the shoulder. "Dan. Dan—we just ain't sure, that's the trouble. We ain't all the way sure, Daniel."

Cutchen laughed a little. "About what, Matt?"

Matt coughed. "I just ain't real sure, Daniel. You can understand that, can't you?"

Harm barked, "Out with it, Matt!"

"Can't, Harm. I *can't!*"

John grew impatient. He faced Daniel Cutchen and he said, "They say my name is your name. They say you are my father."

"That's right!" Matt bawled.

Daniel blinked. Then he took a half step forward and lashed out a fist at Matt Sample. Matt ducked but fell back, reeling off balance. "That's a raw, dirty joke, Sample!" Daniel roared. "One I'd never have thought you'd make. I'll kill the man that taunts me like that again!"

Daniel spun and walked off.

Matt jumped up and ran to catch him. Cutchen tore away from him, pushing him back. Matt talked earnestly, flinging his arms about, swearing solemn vows he was telling the truth as far as he knew. Daniel Cutchen finally calmed down and began to listen. He kept looking back over his shoulder at John. Pulling out a gold locket that he wore on a chain inside his shirt, he opened the square case and looked inside.

He stared at John.

Then Daniel Cutchen started forward, one slow step at a time.

Eleven

Passage of the Sun

On Corn Island, after dark, campfires began to glow, and by one of them sat John Cutchen, his chin resting on his knees, eyes lowered. He was not willing to meet the stare of this man who was his father. He had seen inside the gold locket; had seen a face very like his own, the face of his mother, Marie de Vega Cutchen. There was no doubt of it. The eyes, the chin, the lips—a certain look the artist had captured that both mother and son shared. No, there was no doubt. All the facts of the massacre of Venango, the disappearance of the child, the finding of the body of the man who had carried him over the fort walls—even without the locket, there was no doubt. Daniel Cutchen was his father.

Yet, strangely, John had nothing to say to this man, nothing at all. And Daniel seemed unwilling to press John. He said very little himself at first. But now, sitting there before the fire, he found his voice.

"I was never sure whether you were alive or dead," Daniel said. "Just last fall, before I came with Clark, I carved your name on a grave marker next to where your mother lies. I—I brought her to the wilderness from Boston. She was a sea captain's daughter. He was a smuggler, I guess, bringing in European goods we couldn't get from the British. Tea, woolens, paper, ink— all kinds of things like that—"

"I understand," John said. "He was a trader."

"Well, yes, I guess you could say that. Your mother— well, she was—was beautiful." Daniel rubbed his face. "And me, rough-cut and so certain-sure I could make her learn to love the wilds like I did. Smallpox took her two years after you were born. She—she made me get you away from the smallpox. I took you to my sister at Venango. I guess you know the rest."

"Yes."

Daniel nodded. He took the locket from around his neck and handed it to John. "I'd like for you to have it now."

John took it, then pressed it back into his father's hands. "It is not a thing of me—now," he said. "When I want to see it, I will ask you."

"All right. And if you want to go on calling yourself John Briscoe, that's all right too. I understand. We're still strangers—pretty much."

"Yes, strangers," John said. He stood up with a simple flexing of his legs and glanced at the river. "There is something I must do. Before I sign Clark's paper." He smiled a little. "Matt's wife taught me how to sign my name—John Briscoe. I have only until morning to learn how to sign a different name."

"All right," Daniel said, looking up at him. "I'll help—anything—"

"I will need your pipe," John told him. "And the canoe."

Daniel got up and took a pipe out of his haversack. It was a clay-bowled pipe with a hand-whittled wooden stem. He handed it to John with flint and steel and tobacco. John went down to the shore and was putting the canoe in the water when Harm and Matt appeared at Daniel's campfire. While Matt talked to Daniel, Harm walked over to John at the edge of the water.

"Lad, you ain't gonna run off, are you? Not when you found your real father?"

"No, Harm, no," John told him, smiling. "I will not run away. But I must do something because it is a thing of myself."

Harm applied pressure to John's shoulder. "Listen, John. You've got to tell him about your Injun pa and how it was. How they was gonna make you a chief and all. About the Snake tattoo—all of it. If you don't, there'll be a wall between you forever. You can't give him just half yourself—you've got to give him everything because he's your pa, and because he deserves to know. Once you do that—once you make a clean breast of everything—then you can start a new life among your own kind. But not before. John, don't you know that? You've either got to be a white man or an Indian."

"Harm, I know this. It is what I will do now. I will become a white man. But I must do something, because it is a thing of myself. I do not want you to say anything about my being Indian to him. That is done, so let us forget it." John got in the canoe and picked up his paddle. "I will not run away, Harm. God has sent my father to me, and this is where I belong. I will be here, with you, in the morning."

He dug his paddle into the current, Harm pushing him off. And once he reached the far shore he walked into the forest, carrying the pipe and steel and flint and tobacco until he came to a clearing. A soft light from the moon made the glade seem very still, apart from the campfires on Corn Island. In the clearing he built a low fire, filled the pipe, and sat quietly for a long time.

When the moon was directly overhead, he lit the pipe and offered the stem end up, down, for Earth and Sky. He offered it to the Four Quarters, and held it to the East Quarter last and longest because the east was the source of morning and the morning was the dawn of life. He stood, erect, with his eyes closed and his head tipped back, as he had stood in the council lodge before the Snakes.

"Hear this, my voice, in the silence of the night," he said, speaking low, in Miami. "It is I, Quick Eagle, son of

Blue Heron, come to leave my words with the leaves and on the winds. Hear these, my words, and know my heart. Cause the ones who have known me as Quick Eagle to forget. Cause the sun to shine upon the Miami and his kinsmen. Keep them in good harvest. Bring the warriors victory. Bring the old ones peace. I ask nothing further of life, only this:

"Admit me to that place, when it is time, where I may once again see all those I remember. Let me come upon them smiling where the arrows are sunbeams and the deer do not really die."

He knelt before his small fire and settled back on his heels.

He smoked slowly.

He withdrew his lips from the stem. "My friend, One Fire, thy blood is in me now. I feel it moving upon my heart, and it will be with me all my days. How great a friend you were I did not know. You lied to save my honor when you knew my honor was not worthwhile."

He smoked quietly. "I must think of Feather Wind. Her song echoes to me yet. Surely she will know that I am gone and the song will be heard by another. Be it so that one brings the song back to her in the hollow of his heart."

His lips formed a soft smile. "I must think of my mother. She sent me out each morning in moccasins like my father's own. There were always good things in her morning kettle. More than food, I think."

He put the pipe aside and reached into a small pouch at his belt. He opened a fold of deerskin. He gently parted the milkweed down and looked at what he had revealed. It was Blue Heron's finger.

He smoked. The white streamers of smoke went up and curled around his head and drifted toward the sky. "I remember, my father. Once you told me I did not have to eat the smoke.

"It is not so good within me now, my father. Father, there is no one to comfort me when I feel weak. I miss the stories you sometimes told. Sometimes I grow afraid and lonely and wish that you would come. But you cannot come. Father, I have such a little part of you."

He placed the deerskin with the finger still on it in the fire. He settled back and took up the pipe again. He smoked. "It is well, my father. You shall have a new finger, later. I will bring you one of mine when we meet in the place between the stars and pitch our lodge in the meadows of the Master of Life."

He smoked until the pipe went out. Then he put the pipe on the fire beside the ashes of the finger. He took ashes on his fingertips and touched them to his tongue. "It is filling. It is very filling. When you are with me, my father, I am complete."

He killed the fire with earth.

Then, standing, holding his palm over his heart, he moved his arm away from his body with a long, eloquent, upward sweep.

He said good-bye, and the dawn of another morning was his witness.

He was ready to be a white man.

The day before they were to depart, Clark outlined to his men the journey they were to make and their final objective—the capture and holding of three British outposts: Kaskaskia, Vincennes, and Detroit. In the East the war was not going well for the Colonies, but sudden victories in the West would mean the British could no longer arm the Indians for attacks on Kentucky homesteads. Other settlers would come, making the land already owned more valuable and open new lands for future settlement. The Ohio River would link Fort Pitt and New Orleans, and via the Mississippi the produce of Kentucky farms would find a ready, eager market, cheaply reached.

But that night fifty of the volunteers deserted. Five hundred miles into unknown territory filled with Indians, Tory traders and spies, and British troops held little appeal to them, even in the name of freedom for Virginia and the Colonies. The only future the deserters could see was a death blow from a tomahawk or a British musket bullet.

Nevertheless, on the morning of June 26, 1778, the small army of no more than 175 men started out from Corn Island. The perils they faced were indeed terrible. There was no base of supply. Only a few men would be left on Corn Island, and they could not insure a safe retreat if the army met disaster. The powder was low, the buffalo meat rancid, half spoiled by the summer heat. The French in the Illinois country would outnumber them ten to one—and the French had no idea that, as Clark said, France was supporting the American cause. The Indians, sympathetic to the British, would outnumber Clark's army thirty to one. Clark's least movement would be reported to "Scalp Buyer" Hamilton at Detroit, and Clark could not be sure of continued support by a single man outside himself and a very few others.

Should disaster overtake the army, the Indians were sure to descend in united revenge on the Kentucky settlements. It was five hundred miles to the Mississippi, and beyond that it was Spain. Spain owned the Mississippi River, and the French controlled New Orleans. It was bad enough just taking on the British and Indians. Clark, many thought, looked too far ahead.

It was a grim, solemn group of volunteers who finally poled the flatboats out into the current and prepared to shoot the rapids most generally called the "Falls."

In the midst of the passage through the Falls, the keelboatmen, the volunteers, all became aware of a sullen, ominous silence at the same time. There was the sound of gushing waters, the scrape and click of the poles, and the bleat of a flock of crows that appeared, like doomsday birds, overhead.

Yet for all the sounds, it was deathly still.

The forest on the south and north banks of the river seemed to pause on the brink of a shudder. The river, loud and turbulent, seemed to moan and grieve.

"Look!" a man cried. "The sun! The sun!"

Men looked up. The sun was veiled in a gray, ghostly shroud. A star twinkled beside the gray sun and the land fell away into a hushed, weird silence that lapped over the army like a wave. The men were awestruck. The frontiersman was superstitious, and a solar eclipse became in their thoughts an ominous, foreboding sign.

"Turn back!" somebody yelled. "Back! Back!"

Clark jumped up on the deckhouse of keelboat number one and shook his fist. "It's a good sign!" he cried. "A good omen! It's the eclipse of British power in the West!"

John Cutchen stood with a keelboat pole in his hands, looking up at the sun. His face was convulsed with terror. He dropped the pole and fell against the keelboat railing.

His legs began to falter, and he leaned there, holding on, kicking, coughing, crying, screaming out Miami words.

He tried to hide his face from the sky.

"Aiee! Aiee! My prayer is rejected! I will not go to the Master of Life when I die. He has cast me out! My soul will burn forever in the white man's hell!"

He dropped to the deck, rolling, thrashing, kicking across the planks.

Daniel Cutchen's face was ashen as he bent and tried to pull John up. John screamed in his face, his eyes glazing over as though from death. Daniel slapped him gently. Then slapped him again—hard. "It's a solar eclipse!"

John lashed out at Daniel. "Don't you touch me!" he screamed in Miami. "I do not want to be a white. I do not want to be a white. *I do not want to be a white!*"

He fought free, trying to leap from the keelboat and make his way back to the clearing in the forest where he'd burned Blue Heron's finger. "I must gather the ashes!" he cried, face stricken. "I cannot cut myself off from the Master of Life!"

Daniel Cutchen had to hit him again—hard enough to stun him. John sagged back, and Harm Briscoe, dropping his boat pole, caught him and eased him to the deck. "It's all right, lad! It's all right."

"What's the matter with him?" Daniel shouted. "It's just a solar eclipse. Look—look—it's passing on."

Harm Briscoe gave Daniel Cutchen a pitying look. *"You* know what it is. *I* know what it is. We ain't got soul enough to be afraid of it. But *he* has! Quick Eagle has!"

"Quick Eagle?" Daniel Cutchen asked.

"He's been cut off from his last place to go. He can't get into Indian heaven. He don't just *think* he can't; he *knows* it. Quick Eagle *knows* it."

Harm waved his hand in front of John's eyes. "He's in shock."

"Shock!" Daniel Cutchen said.

"Quick Eagle—" Harm said, smiling at the boy, "that's his Indian name. I ain't never met a man so concerned with his soul before. Why, Quick Eagle just ain't learned yet that everybody is a little impure and imperfect, one way or another. He thinks he's got to be perfect *all* the time. And you want to know something, Daniel Cutchen? This boy durned near is! John Briscoe Daniel Cutchen maybe ain't perfect, but Quick Eagle is! And if I thought it would help him the least little bit, I'd cut his throat where he lays!"

Daniel stared at Harm in shocked disbelief.

"Sounds awful to you, don't it? Well, maybe it is. But I'd do it! Yes, I would! If I thought it would help. But it won't. There just ain't no way to help Quick Eagle now."

"Quick Eagle? . . . What about this . . . Quick Eagle?" Daniel Cutchen wanted to know.

Harm eased John's head to the deck. "He's out. I think

174

he fainted. Well, let him sleep." Harm looked up at Daniel. "While he's asleep I guess I'll tell you about Quick Eagle, Mr. Cutchen. But if I ever hear that you told him I told you, look to your own throat—and I don't care much where you might land!"

Twelve

Kaskaskia

John Cutchen waited by a tree. Powder horn and shot pouch hung under his left armpit, suspended by a cord looped around his neck. His stained buckskins blended with the terrain, and a man might pass within thirty feet and never suspect he was there. He rarely spoke to the plodding volunteers, he seemed oblivious to any discomfort, showed no signs of hunger that beset them all, and he kept almost entirely to himself, squatting there on his heels staring at a fire at night, roaming the woods all day in search of trails and game. He had been farther north than even Clark knew, in search of Indian signs—Miami signs—but he found nothing except a few tracks, weeks old. When the head of the column came up, he signaled Clark that the trail was clear, then stepped back into the woods again, aware that Harm and Matt and Daniel were watching him.

Clark had left the keelboats at the Fort Massiac ruins, and by July fourth the ragged band of 175 men reached a point just across the Kaskaskia River from the town, the westernmost British outpost in the Illinois country. Beyond Kaskaskia was the Mississippi—St. Louis, New Madrid, and the tribes of the western waters, which were little more than legends to these Americans who were twelve hundred miles west of their own country around Fort Pitt.

George Rogers Clark was lying on his stomach behind a screen of ferns, John Cutchen at his side. It was night and in the distance they heard the faint strains of French fiddle music. They could see Kaskaskia from here; the blockhouse of the fort dominated everything.

"Look here," Clark said suddenly, scratching with his fingers in his hair. He held out a pinch of something to John. "Even the lice are bigger out west," he said with a sweet, gentle tone.

"You are quick," John told him. "I have been chasing one the size of a buffalo since nightfall. He has many wallows in my scalp."

"At least," Clark said, "we still got scalps." He sighed, putting the louse, unharmed, on the ground. "I should kill it," he said and smiled. Then in a firmer voice, "Well, John Cutchen, here we are. Now, do you know of any way we can cross the Kaskaskia River there and still keep our powder dry? My scouting around didn't turn up any ford. What about you? Find a canoe cache?"

John shook his head. "No. But why not use the ferry?"

Clark snapped his fingers. "Why, of course! Why didn't I think of that!" He laughed. "What ferry?"

"Upstream a little way there is a man with a flatboat. He poles people across sometimes."

"Sounds handy. But, somehow, it takes the glamour out of it. How many living around the ferry?"

"Just the man and his wife and three children. French half-breeds. My mother was part French."

"I thought she was Spanish?"

John turned his head aside. "Not that mother."

Clark was silent for a time. Then he said, "The ferry-man keep dogs?"

"No dogs. The Pianikishaw Indians eat them. Pianiki-shaw and Miami the same. Same tongue, same people—kinsmen. Like Ogalala and Hunkpapa Sioux."

"Sioux?" Clark asked. "You've seen Sioux?"

"Yes. 'Sioux' is what the Chippewa call them. It means 'enemies.' They call themselves the Lacota—Allies. You can see them, at the fair, the Sioux. A big trading fair, in the West, no white men. The Sioux—they are horse In-dians."

"Eat 'em?"

John smiled. "No. But they like dogs."

"Wonder what dog tastes like?" Clark said.

"It is better than the sour buffalo meat your council of Wise Ones gave you to eat. Dog is better than mutton, but it tastes about the same. It is good, with wild onions. Also with sweet potatoes."

"Mutton. Well"—Clark looked squarely at the boy—

"that's how dog tasted to me, too. I've eaten it. Dog, crow, rancid buffalo meat. Ever eat any crow, John Cutchen?"

"No—o—o." He shrugged. "Maybe."

"Well, maybe Daniel Cutchen has to eat it as a steady diet. He wants to try and know you, John, but you won't let him come close. You won't open up. He wants to help you if he can. I know you had a jolt back there, during the eclipse, but Daniel's suffered too, you know. Why not give him a chance?"

John stared into the darkness. "I will try. Soon. Soon."

Clark nodded. "Well, all right. Now, how about Indians?"

"There are not many now, Colonel. The village is north of the town, closer to the Mississippi. You can hear the French making music, and when they do that the Indians get rum. Also it has been good weather for the buffalo hunting. Tonight, for a week maybe, no trouble with the Indians."

"We'll wait until moonset, then go on over," Clark said, standing up and leading the way back to the knot of waiting officers and men, motioning for everybody to gather around while he drew a ground map.

"Now, men," Clark told them. "Kaskaskia is just over there, maybe a half mile off. We've got to cross the Kaskaskia River, which we'll do on a ferryboat. Remember, we've come to plant the flag of Virginia and the

Continental Congress. By eliminating these outposts, we're going to cut off the base of supply to the Indians who raid our homes in Kentucky. If we hold these posts after we take them, the twelve hundred miles you've just come from Fort Pitt becomes territory you've conquered for your country. All the country drained by the Ohio will become as American as Boston—and that's a land larger than the Thirteen Colonies back home."

Clark tapped his map with a stick. "Now, last spring I sent spies into Kaskaskia. Sam Moore and Ben Limm, here, can tell you what they saw."

Sam Moore spoke up. "What we seen was this: no British troops to amount to anything, a loose-run fort. There's a Frenchy in command, name of Rocheblave, and the British that hired him ain't been paying his wages. The French are scared witless of the Kaintucks and they're not likely to know that France is our ally."

Clark broke in. "We don't want to harm any French citizen—nor any Spaniard that may be visiting from across the Mississippi. We don't want to harm Indians unless they fight. I don't think they will. John Cutchen here says there's a ferry upstream, so let's take it—quietly. Just wave your guns around and show your knives—no killing, but especially no shooting unless absolutely necessary. All you've got to worry about is one man, his wife, and three kids. We don't want to alert the town. Now, men, there's food aplenty in Kaskaskia—just follow the fiddle music to it. But no dancing until the town's ours. That's an order."

"Dang!" said a voice. "And I especially brung my silver buckled dancing slippers."

"Shucks," said somebody else. "I thought you knew, Henry—I ate them slippers two days ago, buckles and all!"

Clark poured gunpowder out of his horn into his hand. "Strip down to the belts, men. Blacken your faces and bodies with powder mixed in water. Any man you see without black paint is against us. And it won't hurt to let the Frenchmen think we're half devils anyway. Any wound you might take on your bare chests will be cleaner and less likely to putrefy than if some of your louse-ridden clothes are carried in with the bullet. So strip to the waist. We can't be sure of a doctor over there."

Clark began to blacken his face. "I want Simon Kenton, Si Harland, Matt Sample, and John Cutchen on the first boatload as scouts. Don't take rifles, just knives. In case of sentries, you know what to do. But once we're all across and you have my signal from the fort walls, whoop and holler like devils. Lord knows, you look and smell like 'em already. Brimstone and what-for, lads! For Virginia and the Colonies. Good luck and God bless you all."

White teeth flashing in their powder-blackened faces, shirts tied round their waists to muffle the clash of hatchet and knife, powder horn and gunstock, the volunteers moved out in a line, heading for the ferryboat.

Daniel Cutchen fell in step beside John, who was spreading the powder-water mixture over his shoulders and arms. Daniel's face was fierce-looking above his heavy beard. "I feel," he said, "I feel like an—Indian."

John smiled to himself. "Sometimes they are painted," he admitted. "But most of the time they are not."

Daniel chewed his lip. "Just when the paint means something, I guess?"

"Yes. When it means something. On certain days." John picked up his rifle, glanced at Daniel, then walked off.

Daniel caught up with him. "Did you hear what Clark said? I mean, about using your knife?"

John looked sideways at Daniel. "It is a war party," he said shortly. "It is war. I am a warrior."

Daniel just nodded. "Well, you're your own man. I just hope we can be friends. I wanted you to know that I'll kind of look out for you if there's any tight places in a fight. I'm asking you to do the same for me."

Suddenly John was sorry he had been so abrupt. He stopped walking. "I am not fair to you," he said. "But once a man told me he wished that I would suffer. He said that by suffering a strong man would be built. He said, too, that suffering sometimes destroyed a man. I have been destroyed. I must take time to rebuild. I must go carefully this time. Many things have happened, things you cannot understand."

"I'd like to try and understand, son. I'd like to help."

John shook his head. "I must do it myself. I must decide myself what I will do."

"If you feel like talking about it, any time, you know where to find me. I'll be somewhere—close."

John hesitated. He stood for a long moment in the dark looking at his father. He reached out and he stroked Daniel Cutchen's arms from the shoulders to the elbows, four times, in love and respect and kinship.

Then he turned and walked away.

Clark's men secured the ferryboat without trouble. A small party of volunteers reported that the ferryman was talkative enough and that they'd only threatened him a little. There was indeed a ball in progress, and Roche-blave, having been across the Mississippi at New Madrid all day, dining with the Spanish commander, did not attend it. He had a habit of retiring early, the ferryboat-man said. There were no British troops in Kaskaskia and none expected any time soon.

The ferry took the men across the Kaskaskia River in four trips. The volunteers assembled in companies on the west bank, lying in the meadow until the moon set and the citizens of Kaskaskia went to bed. The scouts, sent out as spies beforehand, came filtering back. John Cutchen reported that there were no sentries posted on the fort walls, the gates were wide open, and the only person who tried to shout the alarm Matt Sample had tapped on the head.

Clark gave the signal, and like fire-blackened devils the volunteers fell in behind him. They ran lightly over the meadows, through the fields, entered the town, and went through the open gates of the fort. Matt Sample and Simon Kenton were standing by a cabin, waving their arms, and Clark went to them. Kenton said it was Rocheblave's house.

Clark slipped inside, and most of the volunteers with him at that moment followed. Commandant Philippe François de Rastel, Sieur de Rocheblave, who, as Sam Limm had reported, had only a British corporal and a few citizen-militia for troops, was asleep, no doubt confident that things were well in hand.

Kenton tapped Rocheblave on a shoulder with his pistol and the commandant woke up. Clark held a lanthorn above the big pistol in his hand and Rocheblave stared at it. Then he looked around and saw John and Harm and the others and suddenly shouted, "Devils! *Sans doute, sont-ils de vrais diables!*"

Clark's big grin made his blackened face look like a demon's. *"Un coup d'état, n'est-ce pas?"* he said in perfect French while some of the volunteers gaped at him. "And grand *coup,* isn't it? I'll trouble you for your formal surrender of this town and fort, sir," he added.

"Kaintucks?" Rocheblave asked. "Here?"

"Americans," Clark replied. "And your country, sir, is our ally. You are no longer working for the English. I'll be happy to explain that fact in detail, in the morning."

And in the morning the citizens of Kaskaskia peered fearfully from their doors and windows. They had never heard of the French alliance with the American Revolutionaries. But they had heard of Kaintucks and expected to be made slaves, tortured and mutilated perhaps. They huddled fearfully in their homes as the dirty, half-naked, powder-blackened volunteers stalked the streets with long rifles in their hands, wicked hatchets in their belts, and fine French pastry in their grimy fingers.

Clark, sitting in Rocheblave's headquarters, writing dispatches for the East, let the French citizens stew in the sauce of apprehension and fear. He let them fear American soldiery and think what they wished for a time. "I want guards posted on the fort walls," he told Matt Sample. "And I want other men outside town to stop any messages getting through to the British posts at Vincennes and Cahokia. Don't shoot anybody, but stop them. That's an order, Sample. There's no use letting the British know that one hundred seventy-five men took Kaskaskia away from them without firing a shot."

Sample nodded and left.

Clark turned to John. "When I'm done, I want you to carry this dispatch to Corn Island. William Limm will take it east from there. He's waiting in the blockhouse we built on Corn Island. Give it to him, nobody else. Understand?"

"Yes. Yes, sir."

Harm Briscoe was inspecting some of Rocheblave's shelves and cupboards. "Somebody coming, Colonel," he said. "Looks like a committee of citizens and a priest."

The priest came through the door, wearing a frayed, dusty black cassock. He introduced himself as Father Gibault, then introduced the six men with him. They stood back looking at the sweating, powder-smeared Clark as Father Gibault stated their mission. They had come to plead for mercy. The people were afraid and asked to receive God's blessing in church before they were enslaved by the invaders from Kentucky. Wouldn't the Mitchi Malsa grant this request?

Clark raised his eyebrows at John Cutchen.

"It means Big Knives, Colonel."

Clark tossed aside the quill pen he had been using. "Big Knives." He smiled. "Big Knives. Not Virginians— eh? Not Kaintucks or Colonials or savages, eh? Big Knives. A people apart. I like it. But," he added, standing up, "I think you are mistaken about our intentions, Father. We have not come to cause you suffering, but to

186

end it. France is an ally of America, and no interference with religion or families will take effect. Indeed, Father, a new light of freedom shines in the land, and all men are invited to stand in this light, no matter what their race, creed, or color. We would welcome, and appreciate, the support of your people here in the Illinois country. They have nothing to fear from us."

"I am glad to hear it, my son," Father Gibault said. "I have in my keeping many people of the Indian nations. The young men of the village have gone hunting, and some of them ran away when they heard you had come. But the old ones are here and the very young. Those that are left are fearful of what will happen to them. The mothers believe that the Mitchi Malsa keep a pet, a fly, and they think that soon you will turn this fly loose to bite their children who will then have smallpox."

"That is not true!" John suddenly cried. "It is not true about the fly!"

Father Gibault turned and looked at him. "My son, you spoke in the Pianikishaw tongue."

"It is not true about the fly," John said. "I have heard this before, but it is not true. You tell the mothers this."

Father Gibault sighed, lifted his hands, then let them fall. "I will tell them—again." He smiled at Clark. "The people of Kaskaskia know that British-armed Indians, some of them from here, raid the Kentucky settlements. They believe that now you have come for revenge. I hope

187

to persuade them that they are wrong, but the Indians are a different matter. They are—well, hard to reach sometimes."

"It is not true about the fly," John insisted. "My mother was bitten by this fly. It is not just a fly to bite Indians. It is for everybody, all people. Make the mothers believe this."

"*You* make 'em, Cutchen," said Clark. "Never mind the dispatch to Corn Island. This is more important. You stick with Father Gibault. It's an order."

"They'll listen to you, lad," Harm said softly from his corner of the room. "Just show 'em your Snake tattoo."

"I cannot do that!"

"Oh, yes, you can," Harm told him. "It might help save a child or two. Baby you save might grow up to be a Snake himself someday. Besides, don't you owe a kind of debt? You was saved once yourself, wasn't you? Didn't the Indians save you once? Seems that's the way it was to me, anyway. Fella with a Snake tattoo came from nowhere and rescued you pure and simple, didn't he? Then you got raised up good enough to make Snake yourself, didn't you? Ain't that sort of a debt you owe? Seems like if I had ways of paying a debt like that, I'd want to pay it. Sure would."

John made no reply.

Clark noisily cleared his throat. "*Harummm*. Well, our policy toward the Indians," he said to the committee, "is they are free to do as they choose. We hope to establish favorable relations with them by way of trade, but if they wish to fight us, then let them fight like men and we will do the same. We do not seek them as allies in this war, for the Americans do not need others to fight their battles for them as the British do. We desire peace with the tribes, and wish to live side by side with them as the French have always done."

Clark took a turn around the room, hands locked behind his back, while the committee with Gibault watched him. "This is only a part of the army," Clark said, "that you see at Kaskaskia. There is a strong force, quite strong, at Corn Island on the Ohio. If I need this strong force, it is ready for instant service. It should be made known to the Indians that we desire them to lay down their tomahawks and live in peace while we take care of the war we made on the British alone. But if the Indians desire to fight with the British, then they will see their 'hair buyer' fed to the dogs."

John wondered what strong force was at the Ohio River rapids. As he remembered it, only about twenty men were left there in the blockhouse. He wondered if the "strong force" was the kegs of soured, stinking buffalo meat left behind and if that was what Clark meant. It was true that the buffalo meat was part of the army, and if Clark needed it he could bring it up.

Then John saw the faces of the men with Father Gibault and smiled. Clark was being sly. He had to be. Word was bound to reach the British, despite Matt

Sample's efforts, that the American force at Kaskaskia was very small.

The men with Father Gibault were impressed. But John suspected that Father Gibault wasn't, for he smiled at Clark and asked him if Americans believed that confession, now and then, was good for the soul.

"Of course," Clark answered. "And I'm sure that some of my men will be eager to attend church alongside Kaskaskia's citizens."

Father Gibault said, "I could go to Vincennes and help convince French citizens there of your peaceful intentions."

"That's fine, Father. The French as well as any Indian or, indeed, any Englishman who bears no arms against us will be treated with respect, his rights and privileges left intact. Of course," he said, looking at the committee, "I would welcome any Kaskaskia men into the army. They are Frenchmen, and France is our ally."

"Yes," Father Gibault answered. "I'm sure that some of our young men will be eager to become a part of your force. They will join, perhaps, to save—ah—save the expense of transporting other forces from the Ohio."

Clark did not bat an eye. "Quite so. Also it is my desire to call a great council of all the tribes to meet at Cahokia before winter, say, in late September or October I'd like to outline the American attitude toward them as I've outlined it to you."

190

"I am sure they will come. They will wish to see the strength and determination of the Mitchi Malsa who have, after all, invaded a land they consider to be theirs. But by 'all the tribes' do you mean—"

"Yes, yes," Clark said, sitting down and picking up his quill again. "All the Illinois tribes. And Sauk, Fox, Winnebago, Pottawatami, Shawnee, Wyandot, Miami, Chippewa, all—any and all."

John stiffened at the word "Miami" and glanced at Harm Briscoe, who was rubbing his mouth with the back of his hand.

John waited until Father Gibault and the others were gone, then he said he would rather deliver messages and be excused from duty at Cahokia.

But Clark shook his head. "You'd be back from Corn Island by then in any case. I'm going to need you most of all at Cahokia. You don't have to interpret all the time; I'll get a Frenchman for that. I'd just as soon we left the impression we do not understand much of any Indian tongue. But I need somebody to listen—to spy, if you will—to conversations between Indians. I need to know their impressions of us. Pontiac was murdered by whites at Cahokia years ago, and the tribes won't have forgotten it. I need you there."

"The Miami are sworn to kill me!" John cried. "They will kill you too!"

Clark's eyes flashed at him. "I'm not asking you if you

want to go, Cutchen; I'm telling you you are! I shoot deserters if I have to, and I'll shoot you!"

"I cannot help. You will be killed."

"Oh, nonsense," Clark waved his hand. "Indians respect a council. All we have to worry about is right before the council and right after. Besides, we can see how it goes while you are making the rounds with Father Gibault. You've got this far, haven't you? Nobody in the army has been killed. Maybe, just maybe, you're good luck!"

"Yes, sir!" John snapped.

Clark looked at him. "John, John," he said softly. "You can't live in a hut over a hill all your life. Face up to it. Be a man."

"It is not for myself I ask. I ask nothing for myself. I think of Harm and Matt and my father. I think of you!"

Clark made a fist and struck the tabletop with it. "Now look, Cutchen! I didn't expect you to hesitate when I sent you out with a knife in the dark to quietly kill a man who might raise the alarm. I don't expect you to hesitate now. I needed you then, and I need you now! You signed articles of war. Articles of *war*. War is taking advantage of every opportunity and chance you get. It's not just killing; it's spying, trickery, deception—it's lying too. Father Gibault understood that I had to lie! I didn't want to. Well, *war* is a lie, and I hate war!"

Harm Briscoe rubbed the back of his mouth again and stared at Clark.

"Now you, Cutchen," Clark went on. "You help Father Gibault all you can. If just because you're here a child is saved, then that part of the war won't be a lie."

John lowered his eyes. Then he nodded.

"All right then," Clark told him. "Now—now just get out of here. I don't want to hear any more about your personal troubles. I've got enough of my own."

Clark turned to Harm. "You too, Briscoe. Quit rummaging around in Rocheblave's cupboards. I saw that bottle of brandy he left behind. Take a swallow—one swallow—then get out."

Harm nodded soberly. "Thank you, Colonel." He took a swallow and put the bottle back. Then he glared at the back of Clark's head. "Come on John Briscoe Daniel Quick Eagle Cutchen," he suddenly cried. "I'll help you carve your names on your tombstone."

John lifted his eyes. "I am already on one, Harm. My father made one for me. He put it beside my mother, in the East, near Venango. I was living on a borrowed soul all the time. Venango is where I really died."

Clark threw down his quill pen and groaned.

Harm turned and winked at him. "I don't normally drink," he said. "How about you, Colonel, sir?"

Thirteen

Crimson Moccasins

Cahokia, sixty miles north of Kaskaskia, was a small village of French farmers and merchants on the Mississippi just across from the small but growing Spanish town of St. Louis. Like all towns, it had a stockade, but George Rogers Clark scorned the protection of walls and picked a cabin, somewhat off to itself, and with all the insolence of an Alexander or Roman Caesar faced four thousand assembled Indians with less than sixty American volunteers.

The campfires of the Indians Clark had summoned to his council sprinkled the meadows and sparkled in the hills. John Cutchen, scanning with a telescope from the blockhouse of the fort at Clark's order, picked out delegations of Ottawa, Sauk, Fox, Illinois, Kickapoo, Winnebago, Pottawatami, Wyandot, Shawnee, Delaware, and others. He located the traveling skin lodges of the Miami in the extreme focus of the glass but could not determine if the kukewium thrust in the ground before the largest lodge was that of Blue Heron. The Miami had come a long way, west from the junction of the Wabash and

Tippecanoe, and had evidently come with a band of Winnebago, the Puan, whose lodges were mixed with the Miami. The Puan were notably pro-British, and remembering that, John Cutchen frowned. Perhaps the Miami had come, already committed to the British interests.

For three days now Clark had been seeing independent nations, listening to their protests and complaints, threats and opinions, demands and pointless oratory. Clark did not answer questions; he listened, nodding, puffing on the pipes, grunting now and then—never smiling.

The Indians were feeling Clark out, seeing what manner of man the leader of the Mitchi Malsa was, wondering whether he would inspire their admiration or earn their scorn. Clark's stoic attitude left them confused and concerned about what he might eventually say and do. Clark was, in effect, letting the Indians stew awhile, as he'd let the French of Kaskaskia stew and fume and fret, as he'd let his own men do up until the day before the eclipse at Corn Island. Clark was in charge, and the men in his command, as well as the French at Kaskaskia, and now the Indians at Cahokia, could look only to him.

"See him?" Harm Briscoe suddenly asked.

John lowered the glass and chewed his lip. "Stop following me, Harm. Leave me alone."

Harm squinted at John. "Notice you ain't shaved since we landed in Kaskaskia," he said. "You trying to hide out

195

behind that brush—or what? Used to be you kept clean and nice. Now you're as dirty, almost, as me."

John closed the telescope with a snap.

"Let's just say," Harm said, "Blue Heron walked up to you, whiskers and all, and said, 'Come on home, Quick Eagle, and we'll let bygones be bygones.' What'd you do?"

"He will not do that," John said after a moment.

"Let's just say—let's just pretend he's real mad at you for showing up with the invaders and all and asks the rest of the Injuns to jump us and wipe us out. 'Let's revenge ol' Pontiac,' Blue Heron might say. They could do it, you know, wipe us out in a minute or two. And I expect Blue Heron could talk them into it if he wanted to. What'd you do then? Which side would you fight on?"

John gave Harm a scorching look. "He is not a small man! I am nothing to him now. I am beneath his notice. He would not violate a peace council for me!"

Harm spread his hands. "All right. Then let's say Clark asks you to go over there and use your influence on him, on the other Injuns. Show your Snake tattoo and all, like you did in Kaskaskia. Worked there, didn't it? We never got no word of any mothers killing their babies to keep them out of our hands, did we? Supposing Blue Heron forgives you and all, and lets you talk to him. Would you do it? Use your influence?"

"Clark is not such a small man as that!" John cried.

"He is greater than other men. It is not I or Blue Heron who matter. It is a thing between all the Big Knives and all the Indians, not between Blue Heron and me. What is between us does not count here; it is only what is between the two peoples."

Harm Briscoe nodded and grinned. "It took a pretty good chunk of man to say that, John Cutchen. Now, keep what you just said in mind, 'cause Clark sent me here to fetch you. He's ready to see the Miami delegation and he wants you to interpret."

John turned anguished eyes on Harm. "But Clark promised I wouldn't have to! He has a French interpreter!"

Harm shook his head. "Sorry. The Frenchman got drunk last night and hit a lieutenant. Clark's got him in irons until he sobers up. It's an order, he says. You signed the 'listment papers, and you know durned well Clark'll shoot you if he has to. Git down there, lad—"

It was a tense moment for John as he watched the four Miami chiefs walk forward and stand before Clark's small fire. They were Blue Heron, Many Thunders, and the two chiefs who had attended the Snake meeting. Many Thunders handed a black beaded belt, the color symbolic of the state between war and peace, to Clark.

The red belt meant war, the white belt peace. The black one meant that the Miami would listen to what Clark had to say, but the black belt suggested the listening would be done only as a formality.

John was as taut as a bowstring. His nails cut into the palms of his hands until they bled. Twice now Blue Heron had glanced at him, then looked away. His silky black beard must have disguised him; he was taller, thicker through the shoulders; he was in dirty leathers and wore a limp broadbrim black felt hat. Blue Heron didn't know him. After the first glance, Blue Heron kept his eyes on Clark. John remembered the time that Blue Heron had never taken his eyes off the British lieutenant's face either. John wondered what Blue Heron saw in Clark's face.

Blue Heron was not the same. John noted with sadness the lines around Blue Heron's mouth which he had never seen before. His dark eyes seemed weary. And there was the left hand with its four fingers. His straight black hair hung to the small of his back like a horsetail. He was naked except for a Miami short shirt of red wool and old, travel-worn moccasins. No crimson moccasins anymore. John almost wept.

And although there were four chiefs, George Rogers Clark knew instinctively who commanded here, for John saw him looking only at Blue Heron, the merest of smiles on his face. Clark said nothing, only put out his hand to accept the black belt.

"Blue Heron and the nation of the Miami will listen to the Mitchi Malsa Clark, who, though very young, is no child as the British would have us think."

Clark waited. And waited. Then turning, he looked at John. "What did he say, Cutchen?"

But the moment John's voice sounded—sounded out as though coming from a hollow of a cave and a mile apart of himself—Blue Heron turned his face and stared. His dark eyes burned into John's and his whole frame visibly trembled. He seemed to start forward, but Many Thunders touched his arm and Blue Heron drew back. He hesitated, then turned and walked away. Many Thunders gave John a crushing look, then he too turned away. The two other chiefs followed.

John felt ill. Blue Heron hated him. Many Thunders despised him. Their hate might be strong enough to change the Indians' interested tolerance of the Americans into bitter rejection. It might be enough to sway them against the Big Knife whites.

Without waiting for Clark's permission, John turned and stumbled back toward his tent. He walked with his hand before him, feeling his way as though he were blind.

That night, in his tent not far from Clark's cabin, as he tried to sleep, the tribes held dances on the meadow. The drums throbbed and pulsed, booming out a rhythm that matched the pounding in his head. He thought he was going to have the nightmare again, wide-awake, and almost leaped from the bed when a cool hand was placed on his brow.

"They said you were sick," Daniel Cutchen said.

John sat bolt upright. "Do not touch me like that!" he cried. "Never touch me like that. I do not need comforting. I do not need a father! This is not your tent; why have you come? Go! Go now!"

Patiently, slowly, Daniel Cutchen said, "I came to help you if I can."

"Help!" John laughed. "How can *you* help me? Will you find the ashes of my soul and scatter them on my grave?"

Daniel did not try to answer him but took a piece of paper from inside his shirt. "Colonel Clark and I had a long talk about you, son, and we decided that the best thing we can do for you is to let you go. You're no good to us with the Indians, just like you said you wouldn't be. I don't guess I can help you, either. This paper here is what we call a writ of discharge from the Army of Virginia. So you are free to go, son, and I hope you can find your soul again and have—have peace."

John drew a long and tortured breath. How he must be hurting this man, his father. How he had rejected and scorned and failed everyone. He had even failed God, the Master of Life. The Master of Life had surely destroyed Quick Eagle. And now John Cutchen was on the way to destruction too. Had the Master of Life found him so badly wanting? Was he an abomination in the sight of God?

John looked at the paper clutched in his hand. A writ of discharge. Banished. He was banished again and stood alone. Why was he made to suffer so? What had he done? The people on both sides had only shown him love. Harm and Matt Sample and Clark and Daniel Cutchen. Blue Heron and Many Thunders and Rising Owl and One Fire. And for them, for all of them, he had only a knife. He stabbed them and stabbed them until they must cast him out.

John sank back on the bed, eyes brimming. "I—I must be alone. To think . . ."

Daniel patted him on the shoulder. "You think, then. Sleep. Clark will be talking to the counciled tribes, all of them, tomorrow. Then it will be over, one way or another, for all of us."

John caught his father's hand suddenly. "Do not go. Sit with me. Tomorrow we may die. Could I see the locket and my mother's face again?"

"Yes . . ." Daniel's voice trailed off. He cocked his head. "Did you hear something?"

"No, I—" Then John heard it too. He sat up. "Yes. Somebody outside this tent . . ."

"Quick Eagle—" came a choked whisper in Miami.

"One Fire!"

John quickly rolled under the back of the tent, out into

night. He rolled against One Fire. "Oh, my friend. I did not know you were here." He felt for the bumps on One Fire's dear, ugly face, and his fingers, in the dark, encountered something sticky wet.

"One Fire," he gasped. "You—you are hurt!"

"Do not touch . . . knife . . ." One Fire whispered. "It is near . . . lungs . . ."

"One Fire. Who did this!"

"P—Puan. I overheard it. Puan . . . tonight . . . attack the Mitchi Malsa Clark for English pay . . . kill or capture him. You warn . . ."

"Father!" John cried in English. "Warn Clark. Winnebago plan to attack him in his cabin tonight—*now!*"

Without a word, Daniel rose and rushed for Clark's cabin just as musket shots rang out.

One Fire feebly clutched John's shoulder, holding him there. "Brother . . . I die now . . ."

"No! No! I do not wish it!"

"Brother . . . you and I traded . . . blood. I die, for you, brother. Do you know? Do . . . you . . . know?"

John rubbed the tears from his cheeks with the back of his hand. He couldn't see One Fire, and dared not try to touch him for fear of moving the knife.

"Do you know?" One Fire's voice was weak, fading, a hoarse, rough whisper, barely audible.

"I know. I know—"

"Tell . . . me."

"When—when a brother dies for you, then you must live the life he would have lived, with his people."

"Ah . . ." One Fire breathed. "Ah. It is worth it . . . the dying. This thing I do for my chieftain and his son. And for Feather Wind who for a year has been weeping in her lodge. You . . . will honor my death, Quick Eagle? You will honor it? You will not let me die for nothing? You will give him back his . . . finger. Take my name, friend . . . and live my life. You must. I have tricked you. This is my . . . last . . . trick. . . ."

Daniel Cutchen was rushing up with a torch, and other torches bobbed toward One Fire and John in the shadow of the tent. There were no more musket shots, and in the dim light John saw three or four Indians struggling with Clark's men. Clark himself was safe and was striding toward John's tent, shouting for a doctor.

John closed his eyes and knelt over his friend. "I shall honor your blood with all my being, my friend. I am free to go from the Americans, and I shall."

"Ah . . . ah . . ." One Fire said. Then his eyes closed and his arms fell at his side.

A man bearing a torch bent over One Fire. "God," he said. "What an ugly Injun!"

John leaped to his feet, his blood on fire. "He's not ugly! He's not ugly! He's a beautiful man!" He snatched the torch away from the startled volunteer and began beating him with it. He lashed at the man brutally with the burning brand, clubbing him down. And when the man fell, John turned on the others, fully intent on killing them.

Then something exploded on the back of his head and he crashed forward into black nothingness.

Then he was sleeping. And, sleeping, he dreamed. He saw the blood of One Fire spilling, spilling, spilling over him, washing him free. "Ae and ae," he said in sleep. "Red blood. It is the color of a man. One Fire always knew it, but I did not." He swam in ebbing blood in the dream, trying to reach One Fire on another shore.

Then he sat up. "I am coming," he said, "my One Fire."

Daniel clutched him by the shoulder and pushed him back down into Clark's own bed in the cabin. "You've been talking wild in your sleep, son. Rest now. The Indian boy will live. The doctor got the knife out and worked on him all night. His people came and took him at dawn, a few minutes ago."

Live? One Fire would live? A great thankfulness swept over John. He lay back on the pillow and smiled at the ceiling. One Fire would live. "My brother will live," he told Daniel simply. "I see it now. Yes. In the dream the Master of Life wrote the answers that I needed in the blood."

Daniel stared at him, puzzled. "I don't—" He felt John's head. "There doesn't seem to be fever."

John smiled up at him. "I have no fever. I have been visited in a dream by the Master of Life. It has left me weak. But now I have answers. I see that I have been tested for a round, perfect year. I know the thing I must do and how. The Master of Life sent One Fire, my brother, to me. And now I know."

"You mean—you mean you've not lost your soul?"

"I have been made aware of my heart, Father. That is all. It is a heart made up of many bloods, many tribes. My Ordeal before the Master of Life is ended. I come from him naked, like a child. It is all very simple. And I have always known what it was. I will not need the paper of discharge, my father."

"No?"

"I just did not see it with clear eyes. I tried to look two ways with one pair of eyes but could not. But now I have been taught the trick and can see two ways. It can be done more than once in any man's lifetime."

Daniel looked at John with tears in his eyes.

"You will pray with me, my father?"

"Y—yes."

In an hour the great and final council of the Indians was assembled. A fire burned in the clearing before Clark's cabin, and the attentive chiefs looked somewhat fearful of the wrath and rage in Clark's eyes for the

Winnebago attempt on his life. The chiefs were apologizing, and John knew, before Clark opened his mouth, that Clark had won.

A sober French interpreter repeated Clark's words, but John Cutchen interpreted too. His words were understood by the Wea and Eel, the Pianikishaw and the Miami and Shawnee. He addressed Clark's words to Many Thunders alone—Blue Heron was nowhere in sight. Translating Clark's words, repeating them, John looked among the chiefs and warriors, but Blue Heron was not there.

"I am a man and warrior," Clark told the Indians. "I do not care who my enemies are. If you want war, then I give you the red belt. If you want peace, then I give you the white belt. Take whichever one you wish; it makes no difference to me. You Winnebago favor the English and that is your right because you are men and warriors and able to judge who will be your friends and who your enemies. I am not here to ask or beg for peace, but to offer peace and offer war and let Indian men decide what they wish. . . .

"Americans are not a weak people and do not care to have other men, red men, fight their wars for them like the English and French. If we come with only twenty men and not a thousand, it is because we are *men* and do not need numbers to give us courage. . . .

"We are a poor people in our own country. When we

decided to make guns and cloth for ourselves, the English said No! and put garrisons among us to keep us frightened. They said we must buy our guns and cloth only from them, and to teach us a lesson they said a blanket that cost us four beavers before would now cost us seven! And in this way they hoped to keep us forever poor and dependent on them. . . ."

"Now we are still poor, but we are not children and we are not frightened and we are our own nation of men. It makes little difference to us how many friends we have or how many enemies, for we are warriors when we have to be and we can offer peace or war with either hand. It is up to you to judge us and decide for yourselves. You know my thoughts completely. They are the thoughts of the Mitchi Malsa whose big knives are always sharp and in the open so that anyone can see we are not afraid. We are anxious to have peace, but we will not flinch if there is war."

A spokesman for the chiefs said they would council among themselves and tell the Mitchi Malsa, the Big Knife Clark, their decision. They would return when the sun was straight up with either the red belt of war or the white belt of peace. There would be no battle here, on this holy council ground, in case a red belt was given. But if a white belt was given Clark, then the peace would be made by each independent tribe, for each nation must decide peace or war for themselves. And then the chiefs wrapped their blankets around them and moved away.

All but one chief.

Many Thunders came forward and, looking at John, spoke his words to Clark. "My chieftain," said Many Thunders, "has asked me to speak for him and decide with the other chiefs of my nation what we will do. My chieftain, Blue Heron, does not think that peace with the Mitchi Malsa is impossible. In the night a trail of blood was made upon the earth, going from Indian to white, unselfishly. A nation of people cannot be more than its least man, nor less than its greatest man; and let only the Master of Life decide the future. My chieftain, Blue Heron of the nation of the Miami, speaks these words through me."

John interpreted them to Clark. Then smiling, he approached Many Thunders. "Where is my father?"

Many Thunders sadly shook his head. "Gone home. Where you are concerned, he is weak. He could not face you, for he met your white father when we came for One Fire and the two men touched their fingertips together and then they embraced. They could not speak to each other, for Blue Heron is unsure of himself in the white man's tongue and did not want to say something wrong. But they embraced, and I think it was enough to say what they meant."

John almost wept. He turned away from Many Thunders and began walking rapidly eastward.

Clark called after him. "Take my horse, John Cutchen! Be back here before sundown or I'll have you shot for desertion when I catch up!"

John grinned back at Clark. He mounted the horse when Harm Briscoe brought it to him. "Peace now, John Cutchen?"

John patted Harm's hand. "John Briscoe Cutchen. It means 'Good Friend.' Harm, you should have been a Snake."

He kicked the horse in the flanks with his heels and rode away.

He overtook Blue Heron in less than an hour, coming up behind him. Blue Heron was sitting by a gentle stream, the brilliance of the Indian summer forest all around him, the passage of the water over the rocks like the words to a song. Beyond the stream, on a hillside, were several slowly moving figures carrying a litter. One, pausing, waved. John saw that it was Red Panther, helping take One Fire safely home. "Ae and ae," he thought. "Red Panther is handsome and can easily find another wife."

Blue Heron had his back to John, sitting cross-legged with his hunting bow and traveling pack beside him. He half turned when he heard the horse, then flinched and tipped his head forward. His hands, moving rapidly, smoothed out a patch of disturbed sand before his knees.

"So," he said when John dismounted. "So you finally achieved the horse you set out to get. Well, it is skinny. It does not seem to be such a good horse. The price you paid was probably too much."

John smiled to himself. "I wished for a horse long ago," he said. "I did not know that the wish for it was a seed planted in my heart by the Master of Life. The seed he planted, my father, I think will become like a rooted oak."

Blue Heron did not lift his head when John sat opposite him, knee to knee, as in the old times. Blue Heron hung his head. "I am not your father," he said. "Do not call me that."

John smiled down at the stump on Blue Heron's hand. "Yes, you are my father. You paid for me. You paid—too much. But I am glad you paid."

"I am hunting," Blue Heron said. "You will disturb the game with your horse. Whites are not careful enough. Go now."

"I am not white, my father. I am not Indian, my father. I am just myself, one man."

Blue Heron's head dropped lower. John saw drops of moisture strike the smoothed-out sand between Blue Heron's knees.

"Are you weeping, my father?"

"A chieftain does not weep."

John put out his palm and caught a few drops and touched them to his tongue. "It is very good, my father. It is filling. When you fill me, I am complete."

Blue Heron said nothing. His head stayed down.

"Look up, my father, at me, your son. Look at the stream near us, my father. See that there are two sides to the stream, my father, two shores. On both sides there are people, different from one another, but people. My father, there should be a bridge between these peoples so that there is a way to understanding. The Master of Life has made me his bridge, my father. I would be a bridge to both sides, my father. I would be both Indian and white and go among my two peoples to help with other bridges. I would help repair the bridges when the storms divide the peoples, my father. Hear me, my father. I would be a trader and bring the things of both peoples across the bridge. . . .

"My father, listen to me. I would be a trader. From the day of my Manhood Testing, and even before, I thought as a trader and was meant to be one. My mother's people were traders on the Bitter Waters. The horse I wished for was like a seed; and the tree it has grown in my heart will make a bridge between my two peoples. The Master of Life has built me, my father. I was not intended for a warrior. Father, I am only myself. Father, it was hard, very hard, to find this out."

Blue Heron brushed at the sand between his knees,

throwing a handful of it into the stream. "I have seen bridges. The materials in a bridge rot. A child could break a bridge after the rot begins. When you cut down a tree and make it into something it is not, it starts to rot. Sometimes, too, there is ice on the stream and any man may cross. Only the shores endure. A man must live on one shore or the other, not between. On one shore, for you, your father waits, with the whites. Yet upon the other shore a maiden weeps. You would stand between and reach neither of these? Nay, my son. That is bad."

John smiled down at the ground. "Well, Father, I am not perfect. But I love Feather Wind and I promised her that I would come, in my time. I wish you to teach me the words that will win her away from her father. And, my father, if there is a son for me, then you shall have the raising of him while I am among my other people. You shall help me form his soul and shape his heart and bring him before the Master of Life on his Manhood Day. We will teach him to be a man together, my father, and to wear the crimson moccasins I have worn trying to follow in your steps. We will let my son make his own mistakes, as you let me make mine, Father. His suffering will make him strong. But I could wish nothing better for him than that you love him alongside me."

Blue Heron lifted his head, his eyes in pools of shadow under his brow, his cheeks wet with tears. "You see now that I was never so strong as you once believed."

"Ae, my father, you are just a man, with faults, and not a god."

Blue Heron nodded. "So, you have learned something. It would have helped you, this knowledge, when you were chieftain."

"I could not be chieftain, my father. I am not fit."

"You are fit now; you were fit then. But it is too late. The fathers hope for one thing, the sons wish for another. You are going to be a bridge. Who am I to tell you nay?" Blue Heron dug into the sand between his knees and came up with a deerskin bundle. When he had unfolded the wrappings and gently parted the milkweed down that it was packed in, the snake-carved pipe was revealed. "But you are still my son and a Snake."

John blinked in surprise. "You have kept this with you always, my father? Even when you travel?"

Blue Heron shrugged. "I thought I might meet with you in the woods someday."

"You looked for me, my father? Even after the finger, you looked?"

Again Blue Heron shrugged. "I stopped here, my son, to bury you again. But you are hard to kill. Very hard."

John smiled and moved so his knees touched Blue Heron's knees. He leaned forward, white teeth gleaming. "Does the old gray dog still come around, my father? I have missed him very much."

"I have been feeding him, my son. I did not wish to

awaken and have to go alone to the river before the morning meal."

"We will go there together again, my father. It is a good place, perhaps the best place of all, to begin my bridge. You can counsel me about it. I wish to build it right."

"You can instruct me also, my son. So when I lead people to this bridge, they will trust it. So when they use this bridge, they will not fall off and drown in a river of hate."

"I paint your words upon my heart, my father."

Blue Heron held up the pipe. "There is no fire, my son. But this is a pipe my father shared with me, and it is the pipe I would share with you."

"There is fire enough, my father. Between us, fire enough."

"Then, my son, we can smoke."

Quick Eagle took the pipe just on the tips of his fingers. He offered the stem end of the pipe up, down, for Earth and Sky, and to the Four Quarters of the World. He held it to the East Quarter last and longest, for the East was the source of morning and the morning was the dawn of life. He remembered moments of quiet by the river when the cedar waxwing sang. He remembered his wink for the Master of Life that day.

And his eyes closed.

And his heart stilled.

And he prayed.

HARPER TROPHY BOOKS
you will enjoy reading

HARPER & ROW, PUBLISHERS, INC.
49 East 33rd Street, New York, New York 10016